SPIDER
BOY

SPIDER BOY

By Ralph Fletcher

sandpiper

Houghton Mifflin Harcourt
Boston   New York

www.sandpiperbooks.com

The text of this book is set in 11.5/15-point New Aster.

The Library of Congress has cataloged the hardcover edition as follows:

Fletcher, Ralph J.
Spider Boy / by Ralph Fletcher
p. cm.
Summary: After moving to another state, seventh grader Bobby deals
with the change by telling people at school made-up stories
and then retreating into his world of pet spiders
and books about spiders.

[1. Moving, Houshold—Fiction. 2. Schools—Fiction.
3. Honesty—Fiction. 4. Spiders—Fiction.]
I. Title. PZ7.F634Sp 1997
[Fic]—dc20

ISBN: 978-0-395-77606-3
ISBN: 978-0-547-24820-2 pb

Manufactured in the United States of America
DOC 10 9 8 7 6
4500423045

For my brother Tom
who first revealed to me
the terrible beauty of spiders.

Author's Note

Before I wrote *Spider Boy* I did a lot of research in several books. The following three books about spiders are pretty difficult but fascinating:

The World of Spiders by W. S. Bristowe. London: Collins. 1971.

American Spiders by Willis J. Gertsch. New York: Van Nostrand Reinhold Co. 1977.

Arachnida by Theodore H. Savory. New York: Academic Press. 1977.

If you are interested in studying more about spiders, these books might be a good place to start:

Spiders and Scorpions by J. L. Cloudsley-Thompson. New York: McGraw-Hill. 1974.

The Guinness Book of Records, edited by Peter Matthews. New York: Oxford. 1993.

Amazing Spiders by Alexandra Parsons. Eyewitness Junior Series. New York: Knopf. 1990.

Arachnomania: The General Care and Maintenance of Tarantulas & Scorpions by Philippe de Vosjoli. Advanced Vivarium Systems, Lakeside, Calif. 92040. 1991.

One

September 15

I just got a new spider book and the first sentence is: "Spiders are the serial killers, the Jack-The-Rippers, the greatest and most famous predators of the insect world."

This may be true but it misses the point. The incredible thing about spiders isn't that they're killers. It's all the amazing ways they go about getting their food.

People don't understand spiders. They think of them as bloodthirsty vampires. The truth is spiders make the world a better place. They try to give us a bug-free environment. Spider experts estimate that the insects eaten by spiders in one year weigh more than fifty million people!

Spiders are pretty fearless. They eat mostly insects. But they'll also eat fish and amphibians, lizards, young snakes, even birds and small animals.

Most spiders use webs to catch their prey, but not all. Jumping spiders don't use any webs at all. They stalk their prey as slow and secret as a cat. Jumping spiders have awesome eyesight which makes sense—they've got eight eyes.

Tarantulas aren't web spiders. They only use their webs to line the burrows of their hiding places or to keep their eggs warm.

I'm worried about Thelma—still not eating. My book says captive tarantulas don't have to be fed too often. They can go weeks and even months without eating but

"Bobby!"

Bobby blinked and looked up from the journal. "Yeah."

"Time for school! Breakfast! Shake a leg!"

Bobby glanced over at Thelma. The tarantula lay scrunched up and motionless in a corner of the terrarium. She'd been like that for weeks. Ever since Dad got the new job, which meant more money but which also meant having to move from Naperville, Illinois, to New Paltz, New York.

"I'm not hungry," he called to his mother.

"Come on!" she called back. "It's almost quarter of. You better put something into that skinny belly of yours."

Sighing, Bobby closed the journal and tucked it inside the bottom drawer of his desk. He bent down to the terrarium and looked at Thelma.

"So long, girl," he said in a quiet voice. Bobby reached in and gently touched one of the tarantula's legs. "I'll see you this afternoon."

On the way out of the bedroom he slammed into the door. Again! He kicked it, yanked it toward him, and lurched into the hallway. How long would it take before he learned that this door opened *into* the bedroom, not *out* like the bedroom door back in Naperville?

Bobby rumbled down the stairs. Strong breakfast smells in the kitchen: coffee, bacon, frying eggs.

"Morning," Breezy said from the breakfast bar. His sister's real name was Brianna, but a couple of years ago she started telling everyone to call her Breezy. And everybody did except for Bobby, who still called her Brianna whenever he wanted to needle her. Which was about ten times a day. Breakfast for Brianna always meant the same seat within reach of the telephone, the same

3

scrambled eggs and toast, the same Ann Landers column in the newspaper. And now that she was in eleventh grade, a cup of coffee with milk and lots of sugar. A creature of habit.

"How can you drink that stuff?" Bobby asked, eyeballing her coffee. Beneath his belt his stomach made a strangled sound of protest. "Hey, where's Dad?"

"Your father's already at work and I've already done my run," Mom said, smiling at him and sipping her coffee. She was wearing a gray sweat suit with a white headband. "So what are you going to eat?"

"Nothing."

"You can't go to school without breakfast," she said.

"Studies have shown—" Breezy said.

"Studies *have* shown," Mom shot back, glaring at Breezy. "You skip breakfast, you might as well kiss the morning goodbye. Kiss the morning goodbye, you might as well kiss the day goodbye."

"Kiss the day goodbye," Breezy put in, "you might as well kiss your life goodbye."

Bobby stumbled over to the toaster and put in a slice of bread. Ever since they'd moved to New York four weeks earlier he hadn't had much of an appetite.

A car honked.

"That's my exit cue," Breezy said, jumping up. She grabbed her books and kissed her mother on

4

the cheek. On the way out she bent down and kissed Bobby's cheek, too.

"Hey!" he cried, twisting away from her.

"Wish me luck with tryouts!" she yelled. Breezy was auditioning for her high school play, *West Side Story*.

"Break a leg!" Mom called, while Bobby tried to wipe the greasy kiss off his cheek.

*

He stayed quiet during the ride to school. While Mom made small talk (tennis lessons, an argument between two nurses at work, Breezy's tryout), Bobby stared out the window. None of his friends in Illinois had even heard of New Paltz when he first told them he was moving there. It sure looked different from Illinois. He missed the flatness of the Midwest. It was hilly and wooded here in upstate New York, a riot of rocks, bushes, and trees. New Paltz had so many trees you only caught glimpses of sky when you drove around. He missed riding bikes with Mike and Cody and Chad, all those afternoons when there was nothing between them and a huge dome of midwestern sky.

"Bobby?"

He realized Mom was talking to him. She gave him a funny look.

"I said, have you made any friends yet," she said softly.

5

"Nope." He cracked the window an inch; he barely knew any of the kids' names.

"Well, that'll come," she said. "I shouldn't worry about you, should I?"

"Hey, Mom, you're not working today, are you?"

"No, it's my day off. Why?"

"I was wondering if you could take me to the pet shop after school. Thelma really needs a bigger tank. I mean, she doesn't fit in there. She needs to stretch out."

"Don't we all," Mom said.

"I've got the money," he said as they pulled into the circular driveway in front of the school. Mom leaned her head against the steering wheel and looked at him.

"All right," she said. "Now that we've got a bigger house, I suppose Thelma deserves one, too. Listen, I'll be here at two fifty-five on the dot. Don't dawdle."

"Okay." He swung out of the car and waved goodbye.

"Dad packed you an extra-big lunch," she called after him.

"Okay, okay," he said, hurrying into the school. Everything felt different in New York. The air felt strange. His clothes didn't quite fit. Doors didn't open the right way. Sentences, even words, came out sounding all twisted. *Dawdle*. What genius invented a dumb word like that?

*

Bobby had been assigned to Miss Terbaldi's seventh-grade homeroom. When his guidance counselor had first spoken the name, he heard it as *Mr. Baldi*, and it came as a shock the first day to see a woman standing in front of the class. He figured Miss Terbaldi was probably in her forties. She was tall and thin, with bony shoulders bent forward like folded wings.

Bobby took the last seat in the fourth row and watched the other kids filing into the classroom. His school in Naperville had been ninety-eight pecent white; this school had lots of minorities.

"Looks like a healthy mix of blacks and Asians," Mom had said on the first day of school, making it sound like a bowl of human salad.

One boy entered the room slowly, kicking his backpack in front of him. Miss Terbaldi told him to pick it up. He did so, shuffled over to his desk, flopped down, and drew the hood of his sweatshirt tight around his head so his face wasn't visible at all. Another boy, tall with gleaming black hair, strolled over to his desk and shook his head, sending a spray of water from his hair all over the kids sitting around him.

"Mr. Hall," Miss Terbaldi said sharply. "Stop that."

7

"Yes, ma'am," the boy said with a smug smile.

So began the day. The Pledge of Allegiance was followed by the principal's voice running down the day's announcements—the school's placing second in an Odyssey of the Mind tournament, an upcoming Invention Convention, the new honor system, the seventh-grade dance. Bobby tried not to listen.

The bell rang. He walked the halls and went to class like everyone else, as if it all mattered to him. English, social studies, health. Mr. Niezgocki was the math and science teacher. He had a crew cut, and he started each class with a short lecture. Today he talked about "living like a scientist." Then he handed out a thick packet of information with the words CELL DIVISION printed on top.

"This homework is due tomorrow," he said. "If you don't hand it in, I'll put a little zero next to your name in my grading book. All right? When you get two little zeroes, Mom and Dad get a phone call. Is that clear?"

The whole class sighed. It was as clear as it was going to get.

Lunchtime. He ate in the "cafetorium," an enormous room that served as a combined auditorium and cafeteria. Bobby made his way through the line and bought two cartons of chocolate milk. *Cafetorium*, he thought, what a stupid word. Who came up with stuff like that? So far the school lunches had been pretty awful. Today there was a

8

choice between an evil-looking meatball sub and a patty-shaped UFO—Unidentified Fried Object. He felt grateful Dad had packed him a lunch. He grabbed a chair at an empty table and sat down.

"Hey, this is our table."

Bobby swallowed and looked up. He saw a black-haired boy; Bobby recognized him as the kid in homeroom who shook his head like a wet dog trying to dry himself. Two other boys stood beside him.

"Really?" Bobby asked. "I didn't see anybody's name on it."

"Yeah, well, we always sit here," the black-haired boy said, smirking. He was good-looking, with regular white teeth. Bobby took an instant dislike to him. "It's kind of like a tradition."

Bobby looked at them, trying to gauge how much trouble they'd be.

"Mind if *I* sit here?" he asked.

The three boys looked at one another.

"Guess not." The black-haired boy scowled. The other two boys put their trays down at the opposite end of the table and proceeded to ignore him. That suited Bobby fine. He finished lunch and glanced at his afternoon schedule: music, then P.E.

"You're not from around here, huh?" the black-haired boy asked loudly.

"Nope."

"If he's not from around here," another boy put

in, "he must be from nowhere." The boys snickered.

"I'm from Naperville, Illinois."

"You from Illinois?" the black-haired boy asked, making the last part of that word rhyme with *noise*. "You like da Bears, huh? You like da Bulls?"

"I don't watch much sports on TV," Bobby admitted.

"You *don't*?" He looked genuinely amazed. "What kind of stuff you like?"

Bobby shrugged.

"Football. And science."

"Science," the black-haired boy repeated, glancing at his friends. The three of them shared a look before they got up to go.

"Well, see you later, Illinoissss," the black-haired boy said. They started walking away. When they were not quite out of earshot Bobby heard one of them say:

"That geek oughta start saving up his money so he can buy himself a brand-new face." The three of them looked back, cracking up.

*

That afternoon Bobby's mother took him to the library, where he found two spider books he'd never before seen: *The World of Spiders* and *Web of Intrigue*. Next they drove over to Exotic Pets to price terrariums. In one tank Bobby saw a tarantula with beautiful black and orange markings on its legs.

"Sweet," he muttered, his face close to the glass. The sticker on the top of the tank said

MEXICAN RED-KNEE TARANTULA
SALE PRICE: $45

"They make wonderful pets," the man behind the counter told Mom. "Strong but gentle. That one's a feisty little feller."

"You're not thinking what I think you're thinking, are you?" Mom asked Bobby.

"I think I'd better start saving my money," Bobby murmured.

"We already have a tarantula," Mom told the man. "We just need a larger tank."

"I see," he said. "What kind is it?"

"The hairy kind," Mom said. "Lots of hair."

"It's a Chilean rose tarantula," Bobby told him. "A female."

"A good, dependable tarantula," the man said, nodding.

"The only thing is," Bobby said, "she hasn't eaten anything in the past month or so."

"That's not so unusual," the man said. "Lots of tarantulas in here go a month, month and a half, without eating. I wouldn't worry yet."

They looked at five different terrariums before Bobby finally settled on a thirty-gallon tank complete with sand, three big rocks, and a screen top. It soaked up every dollar he had.

"I'd suggest you think about a submersible heater," the man said. "Rose tarantulas thrive in warm, fairly moist conditions."

The heater cost twenty-nine dollars.

"All right," Mom sighed. "We'll take the heater, too. That'll be my contribution."

"Thanks, Mom."

"Nothing but the best for our Thelma," she replied.

On the way home the car began coughing and sputtering just as they pulled up to a red light. Mom managed to get the car restarted, but it didn't go a quarter mile before it started lurching again. Luckily there was a gas station in the next block. They pulled in and found a mechanic to take a look at the car.

"I'll go call Dad," Mom said. She went into the gas station. A minute later, a mechanic came out and jumped into the car next to Bobby. He was young and muscular with a tattoo of a cobra on his right forearm.

"How're ya doin'?" the man said, snapping his gum and turning the ignition key. The engine revved but didn't turn all the way over.

"Pretty good," Bobby said.

"Getting a snake or lizard or something?" the young man asked, motioning at the terrarium.

"Tarantula," Bobby said. "I already got one."

"No fooling." He tried again to start the car. No luck.

"I had a tarantula in that terrarium," Bobby explained, "but it got out about five minutes ago. It's in the car somewhere. They're real good at hiding."

The man froze.

"In here?"

"There's nothing to worry about," Bobby said. "People have the wrong idea about tarantulas. Really. They're gentle pets, not poisonous at all."

Without another word the man got out and backed away from the car without closing the door. Mom stepped out of the gas station.

"Anything wrong?" she asked the mechanic.

"I'm not going back in that car," the man said. "No way."

"Why not?"

"Kid says there's a tarantula in that car! No, ma'am. I'm crazy but not that crazy!"

Mom looked at Bobby. Hard.

"Bobby, you've got something to say to this man, don't you?"

"Sorry," Bobby mumbled. "I was just, like, kidding."

"I can assure you there's no tarantula in the car," Mom explained. "Old coffee cups and wrappers, yes. Maybe even a stale bagel or two. But no tarantula. On that I give you my word. I'm sorry. You know how it can be with a boy's imagination."

"Right," the man said, getting back into the car. He gave Bobby a long, grim look before he tried once more to start the car.

It turned out that the engine trouble was no more serious than three fouled spark plugs. The mechanic replaced the plugs and sent Bobby and his mom on their way.

"Why'd you go and make up a story like that?" Mom asked as they pulled out of the gas station. "You just about frightened that poor man to death."

"I don't know," Bobby said, shrugging. It was the truth: he didn't know.

Two

September 22

Last night I went outside and looked under the porch. There's a big spider living under there— I'm pretty sure it's a marble orb weaver. There was a little green light in its web. When I got closer I saw that it was a firefly, all wrapped up but still alive, its light turned on.

I felt sorry for that firefly, lit up for the last time, but what are you going to do? Everybody needs to eat.

The firefly got me thinking about Mike and Chad and the guys. The night last summer camping out in Mike's backyard when the air was thick with fireflies. His ma gave us empty pickle jars and we caught maybe a hundred fireflies apiece, put them together in one big jar, and brought the jar into our tent. That jar put out so much light we could read comic books!

I really miss those guys.

Last night in bed I couldn't sleep. Started wondering if spiders sleep. I think I read somewhere that they probably don't sleep as we know it. They go through long periods of time where they're inactive.

I got hungry, went downstairs for a bowl of Raisin Bran. In the kitchen there was a little house spider hanging from the ceiling. Not going up, not going down. Hardly moving. Just dangling from an invisible thread.

Exactly like me.

In the morning Breezy was at her command post at the breakfast bar. Mom was sipping orange juice.

"Hi," Bobby mumbled, fetching cornflakes from the cabinet.

"Mor-ning," Mom sang, the first note higher than the other. "How are you, Bobby? Sleep okay?"

"Okay," he mumbled. "You run today?"

16

"Three and a half miles," she replied. "I feel like a million."

He grunted. Sometimes Mom's super-terrific moods were a bit much first thing in the morning. Just then Dad walked in, poured himself a mugful of black coffee, and sat down at the breakfast bar.

"Could I have breakfast?" he asked. "I'd like a cheese omelette, bacon real crispy, and rye toast, butter on the side."

"Ha, ha, ha," Mom said. For the past year there had been a rule in the house that was practically etched in stone: everybody makes their own breakfast. Ever since Mom started losing weight, she never, ever cooked breakfast for the family. She didn't fix lunches, either, and rarely made dinner. Dad did almost all the cooking.

"Joke," Dad said, kissing her on the cheek. "Who needs all that cholesterol, anyway?"

"I do," Breezy said. "I'm an adolescent. My brain is growing."

"That's what you think," Bobby muttered. Breezy had a plate of scrambled eggs in front of her, loaded with black pepper. "Looks like a coal miner sneezed on your eggs."

"Very funny," Breezy said. "Hey, want to hear what Ann Landers said to the woman who married a man who constantly picked his nose in public during their honeymoon? Her advice, and I quote—"

17

"Hey, c'mon," Dad said. "Why don't you pretend this morning that you guys love each other."

"We do," Breezy said. "We fight *because* we care."

Bobby rolled his eyes.

After breakfast he ran up to say goodbye to Thelma. The new tank hadn't made her any more active; she was hunkered down in her burrow at the back. Two crickets jumped fearlessly nearby. Very carefully he picked her up and stroked her legs. He could tell that she liked it when he picked her up. She had a particular way of lifting her legs one after another, and never tried to get away.

"See you after school, girl," he whispered.

Dad had the car going when he climbed into the front seat.

"Some day, huh?" Dad asked. "Look at that sky! Look at those leaves! We never had a fall like this in Naperville."

Bobby snapped the seat belt into place. In Naperville the cornfields turned brown in autumn. But on certain overcast days he'd be playing tackle football with a bunch of guys in the Worthens' cornfield when all at once the clouds would break enough for the sun to peep through. At a moment like that the whole cornfield would be shot through with gold.

Now that's fall.

Bobby looked out the window. He hated it

here. He would never get used to all the hills, the rocks, the tree-covered sky.

If you're not from around here you must be from nowhere.

That just about summed it up.

"I won't be able to give you a ride home after school," Dad said. "You be all right?"

Home. For the past few weeks when people said anything to him, Bobby often heard words, not out-loud words, but words in his head. This time those head words said clearly, *Home? Home is about eleven hundred miles from here.*

"That's okay," he said. "I don't mind walking."

*

The school day passed slowly. Classes droned by. When the bell rang, Bobby collected his books, got up, and walked down the halls. It felt like moving in a dream.

After school he hurried home and went upstairs to check on Thelma. She was lying at the back of her cage exactly as he had left her. He wanted to pick her up again and play with her, but something told him to respect her privacy. Leave her alone.

The phone rang. It was Mom calling from work.

"How was school?"

"She's still not eating, Mom," he told her.

"Who?"

19

"Thelma." *Who do you think?*

"I know you're worried," she told him. "But try to be patient. The man at the pet store said it's not unusual for them to stop eating for a while, right?"

"Yeah, I know."

"I'm sure she's going to be fine," Mom said.

After Bobby hung up he went to his bedroom. He looked around at all the boxes containing his stuff, the posters still rolled up. It looked like he'd just arrived yesterday. The only things he had unpacked were his clothes and a few books. The room was long and narrow. With the walls bare, you could see that they needed a paint job. There were four windows, each shaped like a quarter of a circle. Those windows, Mom said, gave the room character. Four quarters equals a whole. But it didn't add up.

He lay back on his bed. The house was perfectly quiet, as if all human sound had been sucked forever from those four walls. Bobby felt his stomach rumble.

"Bandersnorple," he whispered. One of the secret code words he and Mike used to prevent other people from intruding in their conversations.

"Bandersnorple!" Mike would yell to him from the other side of the crowded town pool. All the kids around him would look at them like they were crazy. They had no way of knowing that *bandersnorple* was code for *I'm-starved*. He and Mike had lots of secret words like that. *Sasparilla* was code for *I've-got-gum-you-want-some? Sergio* meant *I'm-bored-let's-get-out-of-here.*

"Sergio," he whispered. He'd never been so bored. But where could he go?

The phone rang. Bobby sprang off the bed and ran into his parents' room to answer it.

"Hello?"

"Hey, Bobs! It's Mike!"

"Mike! I was just, like, thinking about you!"

"I told you I was going to call today. September twenty-two, remember?"

"How could I forget? How ya doing?"

"Okay, I guess," Mike said. "Bored silly, tell you the truth." Bobby heard Mike blow his nose. "Stayed out of school today—flu."

"Oh yeah?"

"Yeah. Ever watch daytime TV? It really sucks. All the commercials are about diapers and laundry detergent."

"Yeah." Bobby laughed. For a moment neither one of them said anything. "Hey, you playing football?"

"Little. I signed up for travel soccer, so that's keeping me pretty busy on Saturday."

Bobby stood in his parents' bedroom, the phone glued to his ear, hardly paying attention to what Mike was saying. It was enough just to let the sound of Mike's words roll over him. He pic-

21

tured the words streaming between Mike and himself, words stretched along a single thread, the only thing connecting Bobby to the real world.

"How's Thelma?"

"Great!" Bobby told him.

"Really?"

"Listen to this," Bobby said. "The woman from next door came over to visit, right? I was playing with Thelma on the kitchen floor. Thelma started running toward her and this lady totally freaked!"

He could hear Mike laughing.

"The lady was having heart palpitations!" Bobby said. "They had to call an ambulance!"

"Ha!" Mike started laughing even harder.

"I'm telling you!" Bobby finished laughing and took a deep breath. "And Thelma's been eating like crazy! I mean, she devours everything I throw in her tank! Totally bandersnorple."

There was a short pause.

"Oh, right," Mike said. "Hey, wow, well that's good."

Another long pause. Bobby tried to think of something to say.

"I guess I'd better go," Mike said at last. "I'm sending you a letter so write back quick or I'll rip your head off."

"Okay, okay," Bobby laughed. "Hey, say hi to Chad and the guys."

"Okay, and don't forget—next time it's your turn to call me. A month from today, except I might be away that week. Better make it October twenty-eight. Write it down."

"I will." A month seemed like forever. "October twenty-eight, four o'clock."

"Right," Mike said. "Wait a sec. Is that four o'clock your time or my time?"

"Well, I dunno," Bobby said, confused.

"Better make it four o'clock my time," Mike said. "Five o'clock your time. Okay?"

"Okay."

"Bye, Bobby."

"Bye, Mike."

He walked back to his room and glanced down at Thelma sitting in her new tank. Bobby sat on his bed trying to sort out his feelings: happy, lonely, a little sorry he had made up those stories about Thelma. But there was something about the conversation that bothered him. *Is that four o'clock your time or my time?* He'd always pictured himself and Mike together, breathing the same air, going through the same time. It had never occurred to him that their time zones were different now that he had moved east. The thought depressed him.

"Should've done this weeks ago," he whispered to Thelma, looking at his watch. He went to work and changed both his wristwatch and alarm clock from 4:05 eastern daylight time to 3:05 central daylight time.

Three

September 24

The web is what makes spiders different from other bugs. The web has always been spiders' major weapon in their war against insects. Some scientists believe that millions of years ago insects developed wings so they could fly away and escape from spider predators. But spiders fought back—they evolved the use of silk webs so they could catch those flying insects.

Just a theory but it makes sense.

Most spiders like to spin their webs either at night or in the early morning. Some spiders eat their webs at the end of the day and make a new one the next morning.

People have found lots of uses for the silk from spider webs. Optical instruments, for example. The crosshairs on rifle telescopes used to be made of spiders' silk.

Some webs are amazingly strong. People have gathered the web from the Nephila spider and used it to make fishing nets. The silk has even been woven into fabric.

For a long time people used cobwebs to stop the flow of blood on a wound. Even now people who clean out horse stables are told not to clear away the cobwebs because "you never know when you might need them."

All through history there have been people who believed there was something magical about spider webs. I read that in Kentucky some people still believe that President McKinley's death was prophesied in spiders' webs.

Also read that people in North Carolina in 1914 and again in 1917 reported that they saw lots of Ws in the webs of garden spiders. They thought the Ws stood for the initials of Woodrow Wilson. Or World War I.

Which reminds me—I HOPE we don't have to

read Charlotte's Web *in English this year. We studied it last year in Mrs. Sibberson's class, and I've read the book at least five times on my own. It's a good book—well, all right, a great book— but I'm a little sick of it.*

It's not just that silly stuff about how Charlotte writes SOME PIG in her web. What bothers me is the way the book makes Charlotte seem so nice and kind. There's nothing nice or kind about spiders. They are killers. One author calls tarantulas earth tigers. They're merciless. There's no room for mercy when it comes to survival. When you're trying to survive, you have to look out for Number One.

In school Bobby drifted alone through another boring day: English, social studies, health. In science class Mr. Niezgocki assigned the essay topic: "How Science Affects My Life." The other students opened their notebooks to blank paper. In the front row, the boy from homeroom with the slick black hair groaned and rolled his eyes. Chick Hall, that's what Mr. Niezgocki called him yesterday. What kind of a name was that?

Bobby sat there, thinking. Writing didn't scare him like it did some kids. But what to write about? He could write about his mother's job as a nurse—strep tests, HIV, AIDS, blood cell counts, meds. Dad's job making cardboard containers probably involved science, though he didn't know much about it. He could try something ordinary—TV, refrigerator. Or maybe the car, those fouled spark plugs. Blah blah blah . . .

All at once he sat up straight; his pen started scurrying across the page. The words came fast the way they often did when he wrote in his spider journal, and he had to work quickly to get them onto the paper. Pretty soon he'd filled up all of one page and most of the back.

"Stop!" Mr. Niezgocki said sharply. "Even if you're in mid-sentence. Even if you're in the middle of a word. I know most of you aren't finished yet. You can finish these tonight. Right now let's hear someone read what they've written. Out loud. Any volunteers?"

Bobby's hand shot up.

"All right." Mr. Niezgocki smiled at him. "You're . . . Robert Ballenger, right?"

"Bobby," he said.

"Okay, Bobby, go ahead. Please stand. You don't have to come to the front of the room, but I would like you to stand so everyone can hear."

He stood, his chest like a straitjacket around his thumping heart and began:

SILK FARMING

My father is a silk farmer. For the past

27

ten years my dad has run a silk farm in Naperville, Illinois. It's a fairly large farm—a hundred and ten acres. This farm has been so successful that my father wants to expand. He is looking at some places in Arkansas where the land is cheaper.

Silk is a kind of fabric that people will pay lots of money for because of how it feels against their skin. Silk sheets feel cool on hot summer nights, but a silk shirt will keep you warm when the weather turns cold.

My father just may run the most unusual silk farm in the world. Most silk gets produced from silkworms, in Asia. The silk comes from the cocoons of the silkworms. But the silk on my father's farm is made from spiders, from their webs. And spider silk is so soft and strong and light my father can charge a high price for it.

You may be wondering, If silk from spiders is such a great idea how come nobody else thought of it before? Well, they have. Many people have tried to mass-produce spider silk. But here's the problem. Unfortunately, spiders are cannibalistic. They have a nasty habit of eating each other.

Bobby glanced up and saw the other kids listening intently.

This was the biggest problem my dad faced and here's how he solved it. He found a special chemical that makes spiders less aggressive toward each other. But the next problem was how to get the chemical into the spiders without disturbing them.

My father tried lots of things, but none of them worked. Finally he found an answer. He sprayed the chemical on sugar and fed this sugar to the flies. (He also raises houseflies by the millions to feed the spiders.) When the spiders ate the flies, the chemical made them much calmer. Now they hardly ever eat each other.

He stopped and looked up.

"That's as far as I got," he said.

"That was good!" one boy said.

"Nicely done!" Mr. Niezgocki said, nodding. "You included some strong supporting details. Any questions or comments for Mr. Ballenger?"

"Is that stuff true?" a boy asked. "About spiders being cannibals and stuff?"

"Yes," Bobby said. "Sometimes the females will eat the males."

"Smart," one girl said, nodding. "Serves 'em right."

"I hate spiders!" another girl said. "And my grandma is worse. Mom makes us kill all the spiders in our house because she's afraid if

Grandma even *sees* a spider she'll die of a heart attack."

"Can you bring in some silk made on your farm?" The question was asked by a tall girl on the window side of the room. "I'd love to see some."

"I'm not sure," Bobby mumbled. "Maybe. I'll see if I can find any around the house."

"Okay, okay," Mr. Niezgocki was saying. "I'm looking forward to reading the rest of these. For homework I want you to finish up these essays and hand them in tomorrow. No excuses. You don't hand them in, and I put a little zero by your name. Is that clear?"

*

In the cafetorium Bobby took the same seat at the same table as the day before. He opened his lunch bag. As usual Dad had packed way too much food: olives, cut-up veggies, pickles, crackers with peanut butter, a ham and cheese sandwich, brownie. He kept the food in his lunch bag so nobody would see.

Chick Hall and his two friends took seats at the other end of the table. They ignored him. Ten minutes later a skinny boy took a seat at Bobby's end of the table.

"Hey, if it isn't Fostick the worm!" Chick said to him. "What rock did you crawl out of, huh?"

The skinny boy just shrugged and started eating: bologna with mayo on white bread.

"The spider man!" Chick Hall looked over at Bobby, nodding. "Hey, pretty cool story you read today. You know a lot about spiders, huh?"

"I got lots of books on them," Bobby admitted. "And I've got a pet tarantula at home. It's like a hobby with me."

"His family's got a spider farm in Illinois," Chick said to his friends.

"Spider boy!" one kid said.

"Yeah, the spider boy from Illinois!" Chick said, slapping the table. One of the kids started to laugh with food in his mouth, which got him choking. Chick stood up and started pounding the boy's back.

"I'm okay, I'm okay!" the boy said. He took a swallow of chocolate milk and gave Bobby an evil grin. "The spider boy from Illinois. Perfecto!"

"Thank you, thank you," Chick said, standing and bowing formally to the right and the left. He started singing to the tune of the *Spiderman* cartoon on TV:

> "Spider boy,
> Spider boy,
> Spider boy from Illinois . . ."

The three of them drifted off, singing and roaring with laughter, leaving their lunch trays on the table. The skinny boy looked at Bobby.

"Friends of yours?"

31

"That one kid is in some of my classes," Bobby said.

"Chick Hall," the boy said, nodding. "He's pretty much a jerk. He works hard at it. And believe me, it takes a lot of practice to be such a pain in the butt. Teachers let him get away with it. I think it has a lot to do with him being on the swim team. I have a theory about teachers and jocks—basically any athlete can get away with murder, especially the good ones. Chick swims a mile every morning. He's ranked number one in the state in the under-thirteen group."

Bobby shrugged.

"His father was an Olympic swimmer. And his big brother, Luke, swims on the high school team. Check out that shirt Chick is wearing?"

Bobby shook his head.

"Take a good look. Yale swim team. Luke Hall's an *awesome* swimmer. We're talking All-American. We're talking full scholarship to Yale. The whole family has webbed feet. And they're all pretty much jerks, the way I hear it." He pointed at his head. "All that swimming tends to make the brain a little soggy. That's basically my theory about swimmers."

"Have you got a theory about everything?" Bobby asked.

"Basically," the boy said.

"Is Chick his real name?" Bobby asked. "What kind of name is that?"

"His real name is John," the boy said. "But everyone calls him Chick. He saved a guy's life last summer, you know."

"Yeah?" Bobby was interested, despite himself.

"Yeah. This big kid, Ricky Horn, he was swimming at the lake and got a bad cramp and started going down for the count. Chick swam out and dragged him back to shore. Ever since, he's been strutting around like he's God's gift."

"I've known guys like him," Bobby said, thinking of two conceited guys back in Naperville. Some things don't change no matter where you live.

"In this school," the boy was saying, "about ninety percent of the kids are obnoxious jocks, stuck-up girls, nerds, geeks, or basic jerks."

"And I guess you're in the other ten percent," Bobby said.

"Are you kidding? I'm captain of the chess team. Which pretty much makes me the biggest nerd in the school."

"Oh," Bobby said. They both laughed.

"I'm Butch Fostick," the boy said.

"Bobby Ballenger."

"Nice to meet you. Play chess?"

"Not much," Bobby said.

"Let's do a game," Butch said eagerly. "Pawn to king four."

"I give up," said Bobby, throwing up both hands.

33

"We'll play sometime. I can teach you stuff. I know this nasty five-move checkmate. People walk right into it every time. You're from Illinois, huh?"

"Yeah."

"Right. The spider boy from Illinois." Butch shook his head. "You know, that nickname just might stick."

"Yeah."

"Listen," Butch said, picking up his tray. "Whatever you do, don't let Chick Hall get under your skin. He's just testing, you know? Stay cool and pretty soon he'll give up and find some other lucky kid to torture."

Bobby nodded.

"You know your watch is wrong," Butch said. "It's an hour off."

Bobby glanced at his watch: 11:58. In Naperville it was two minutes until noon.

"Yeah, you're right," Bobby said, though the voice in his head insisted, *Oh no it's not.*

Four

September 27

Mike sent me a letter with a whole list of cool facts about spiders:

The biggest spiders in the world are the gigantic bird-eating spiders from Guyana in South America. In 1985 they found a spider with a 10 1/2 inch leg span. This sucker had a body that weighed about 4 ounces. Its body was 4 1/2 inches long with fangs 1 inch long!

The smallest spider in the world is the Patu marplesi *from Western Samoa. It measures just about the size of a period in a book.*

The most common spiders in the world are crab spiders.

The rarest spiders in the world are the trap-door spiders found in Southeast Asia.

Tarantulas live longer than any other spiders in the world. It's not uncommon for females to live for 25 years. Males usually die younger.

The fastest spiders in the world are the African long-legged sun spiders. They need to run fast to eat geckos and other desert lizards. They can run about 10 miles an hour.

The biggest webs are made by the tropical orb weavers (Nephila)—they spin webs up to 18 feet long!

The world's most poisonous spiders are the wandering spiders (Phoneutria) from Brazil—big spiders that hide in clothes and shoes and can bite furiously when disturbed. Luckily, scientists have an antidote for the poison.

I know Mike got most of these facts from the Guinness Book of World Records, *but they were still fun to read. He wanted to know all about New York, and how Thelma's doing. She's still moping around. Hasn't touched the fresh crickets I bought for her.*

Mike's letter made me feel weird. He wrote about

going camping and going to Wrigley Field to see the Cubs. Playing football on Saturday, watching a video, riding bikes with Chad. Last Sunday they got 10 kids together at his house for a big game of "killer croquet." He and Matt and Chad all got on the same travel team for soccer. Funny— it's not the special things he told me about but the normal stuff that made me homesick.

In homeroom Bobby found a sign in heavy black lettering taped to the top of his desk:

WELCOME TO
SPIDER BOY
FROM ILLINOIS!

Bobby calmly took the sign off his desk and sat down. A minute later Chick Hall came running in.

"Hey, Spider Boy!" Chick called from the other side of the room. "How d'ya like that sign, huh?"

Bobby ignored him.

"Yo, Spider Boy!" Chick called again. "Hey, *scuuuuse me*, Spider Boy!"

Bobby forced himself not to turn around.

"Mr. Hall," Miss Terbaldi said. "Please lower your voice."

"But he's Spider Boy from Illinois," Chick said in a smirky, nerdy voice. "That guy's wicked awe-

37

some cool! I wanna get his autograph! He's, like, a celebrity!"

A few kids laughed; Miss Terbaldi frowned at them. With her bony shoulders bent forward, she really did resemble an old eagle.

"That's quite enough," Miss Terbaldi said.

"But Miss T, his best friends are spiders!" Chick said.

"Enough, Mr. Hall!" Miss Terbaldi stood in front of him. "You have disturbed this class enough for one day. One more outburst and you can spend the day with our assistant principal."

"Good morning, girls and boys." The voice of Mr. Wagner, the principal, came booming over the intercom. On alternate days he began his announcements "boys and girls" and "girls and boys."

"Please listen for the day's announcements. In less than two weeks, as you know, we will be trying an experiment with the honor system here at Regina White Middle School. The honor system will put more responsibility on each one of you."

The voice droned on. Nobody in class seemed to be paying attention. Bobby half-tried to listen, but his thoughts kept floating back to Naperville—Mike, Cody, Chad. After Mike's letter he could think of little else. Mike's family had lots of money; he lived in a mansion with a humongous backyard. Every Saturday morning all the guys got together to lay down a regulation-size football field at Mike's house. They used real lime to mark the lines, and afterward they played tackle football. Sometimes twenty kids showed up to play. The games lasted for hours, and everyone always went home with ripped clothes, bruised and happy.

The bell rang; kids jumped up.

"Hope I'm not *bugging* you, Spider Boy!" Chick Hall called on the way out of the room.

Bobby glanced down at his watch: 7:20 A.M. In Naperville, school hadn't even begun.

In English class Miss Terbaldi gave a lecture about the short story. Conflict and resolution. Characters, plot, setting. But the only setting Bobby could picture was his bedroom on the third floor of their house back in Illinois. In the long crawl space behind his bed he had set up a whole system of boxes for his fossils, arrowheads, crystals, and baseball cards. The room had two windows that overlooked a patch of woods. On certain nights the moon rose over those woods and threw slanted arrows of silver light into his room.

In science, there was an assignment written on the board. SHORT ORAL PRESENTATION.

"You're going to choose a topic of interest to you," Mr. Niezgocki explained. "This is not a big deal. These will be short, five to ten minutes, maximum." He underlined the word *short* on the board. "These will be due next Monday. Next week we'll spend time in class listening to the presentations."

"Can we work with a friend?" a boy asked.

"Let me finish," Mr. Niezgocki said. "Yes, you will do your reports with *one* person. Please get together with a partner."

There was a wild scramble as everyone started pairing up. Bobby sat watching.

"Need a partner, Mr. Ballenger?"

Bobby looked up and saw Mr. Niezgocki smiling down at him. A tall girl stood beside him.

"Do I?" Bobby asked, shrugging.

"You do," Mr. Niezgocki said. "And by coincidence, Lucky also needs one. Bobby, this is Lucky. It turns out you are both new to the school. Why don't you work together?"

"Okay," the girl said in a low voice. She didn't seem thrilled about it.

"Yeah, all right," Bobby mumbled. The voice in his head said, *Just my luck.*

*

After class Bobby pressed into the mass of students heading for their lockers. And home.

"There he is!"

He looked up. Chick Hall.

"Spider Boy from Illinois!" Chick said, grinning. "I can't believe I'm actually talking to him! Can I have your autograph? Please?"

40

Bobby walked up to him. He took out a piece of paper and scribbled his name on it.

"Here," he said, handing it to Chick. "My name is Bobby Ballenger. In case you're interested. B-O-B-B—"

"Mr. Ballenger!"

They looked up. Mr. Niezgocki. He took Bobby by the arm and led him away while Chick Hall madly waved after him.

"I'd like to speak to you for a moment. Here."

He led Bobby through an unmarked door and shut it. Inside, the only sound came from two aquariums bubbling along one wall. Bobby counted five terrariums on the other side of the room. There was also a mass of green plants under bright lights.

"Hope you didn't mind me pairing you up with a stranger today," Mr. Niezgocki said.

"I don't know anybody in this school," Bobby said with a shrug.

"Did you two pick a topic yet? For your report?"

"Not yet." He shuffled his feet.

"Just don't leave it until the last minute," Mr. Niezgocki said, leaning back against one counter. He was a tall man, much taller than Dad, with a deeper voice. He had reddish hair and glasses. "Say, that was some essay you wrote Friday about your father's silk farm."

"Thanks," Bobby said quietly. He turned to

watch two fish—black angels—chasing each other in one of the aquariums.

"You sound like quite an expert."

"I know stuff about spiders," Bobby said. "It's kind of like a hobby with me."

"Really." Mr. Niezgocki nodded and crossed his arms.

"Yeah, well, I have a tarantula at home. A pet. And I've read a bunch of books about spiders."

"Spiders are fascinating," Mr. Niezgocki said. "I've done some reading on them myself. Some of their survival mechanisms are ingenious."

"I keep a journal," Bobby said. "Like a science journal about spiders."

"A spider journal. That's interesting. I'd love to read it."

Bobby blinked. He had never imagined letting anyone read the journal.

"Well, parts of it are sort of personal."

"I see," Mr. Niezgocki said. "Well, you could just show me the scientific parts. Say, I haven't shown you around my office, have I? Let me give you the tour. These aquariums are for tropical fish. Last year I bred Siamese fighting fish in this one, and I'm hoping to do it again this year. The conditions have to be exactly right—pH, water hardness, temperature, salinity, everything. You know how it happens? The male makes a bubble nest in one corner of the tank. When the time's right, he wraps himself around the female, squeezes the eggs out of her, and blows them into the nest. It's the male who tends the eggs."

Bobby leaned down to peer inside a terrarium; a green lizard glared back at him.

"I'm pretty interested in tarantulas myself, but we don't have any here yet, unfortunately," Mr. Niezgocki said. "That lizard you're looking at is a gecko. I'm planning to get a snake or two as well."

He rubbed his chin.

"You know, I could use someone to help take care of this lab after school. Feeding, cleaning cages, putting stuff away. Do you have any interest in a job?"

"I don't know," Bobby said.

"I'm thinking of maybe three hours a week. The hours would be pretty flexible. I'd pay you, of course. We could work out a fair hourly wage."

Bobby looked down into the empty aquarium.

"You could even bring your tarantula in here if you'd like," Mr. Niezgocki said.

"Really?"

"Sure. That way you could see her during the day." He glanced at his watch. "Think about it. We can talk more tomorrow."

Five

Spiders lie. Well, not exactly lie. But some spiders change what seems to be true by pretending to be something they're not. And isn't that what lying is all about?

They do it through camouflage. Some spiders can change to look like the bark of a tree. This makes them invisible to birds and other predators.

There is one spider that imitates an ant. Other ants don't get scared when the disguised spider comes near. When it gets close enough, it pounces.

A certain kind of crab spider can make itself look like the stamen on the inside of a flower. A bee sees it, flies in and—WHAM! Supper time.

Spiders lie, all right, but there's a good reason for it, the only reason animals do anything: Survival.

Lying was easy. Simple. You could tell people all sorts of fake stories about yourself, but if you told them with a straight face, well, people would believe you. Especially if you had just moved to town from another state, with no way for people to check whether or not you were telling the truth. This was maybe the only advantage to being the new kid in town.

It amazed Bobby how easily everyone swallowed the tall tale about the spider silk farm. Afterward he felt funny about it, the same way he had felt after lying to Mike about all the amazing things Thelma had been doing. It was wrong, and he told himself he had to stop making up stuff like that.

On Tuesday Miss Terbaldi talked to him after English class.

"I've been wanting to welcome you to New Paltz," she told him. "You moved here from Illinois, right? What brought you here?"

"Spiders," he said. Miss Terbaldi looked surprised.

"What do you mean?"

"My dad just took a job as director of the spider department at the Museum of Natural History in New York City. That museum has just

45

about the biggest collection of spiders in the world." Bobby knew that this was true—he had just read an article about it. "Over a million different specimens. Keeping track of them all is a pretty big job. My dad's got a dozen people working for him."

On Wednesday he told the librarian that his father trained dolphins for a living.

"Really!" Mrs. Nederhauser gave him an enormous smile. "You know, I have always dreamed of working with dolphins. Fascinating creatures! So friendly, and so intelligent!"

On Thursday, during homeroom, Bobby got a call to report to the Guidance Office.

"Uh-oh," Chick snickered. "Disaster for Spider Boy!"

At Guidance, Bobby expected he would meet with Mr. Carney, the advisor who had given him his schedule on the first day of school. Instead, a young woman came out and ushered him into her office. Posters of rock stars and surfers on the wall. The gold nameplate on the desk read JENNIFER DAVENPORT. Miss Davenport had California blond hair and a California tan, to boot. Very pretty. But Bobby didn't trust anybody who looked like they'd just popped out of a fashion magazine. She gave him a huge smile with straight white teeth. *Somebody*, he thought, *must've shelled out megabucks for teeth like that.*

"Aren't I supposed to see Mr. Carney?" he asked.

"We've shuffled around some students, so from now on I'll be your guidance counselor," she said. "How's your year going?"

"Okay," he said. Another lie. Easy.

"Any problem with your class schedule?" Miss Davenport asked.

"Nope, it's fine." Bobby glanced at his watch. Seven forty-eight in Naperville. He pictured Mike at that moment, chowing down on a huge bowl of cornflakes. "Can I go now?"

"Not yet," she said, giving him another high-watt smile. "I wanted to introduce myself to you. I want you to think of me as someone you can talk to. You know, if something's bothering you."

Terrific. He nodded without looking at her.

"You're new to the school, right? Mrs. Nederhauser tells me that your father trains dolphins for a living . . . ?"

"Yeah, sort of," Bobby said.

"Sort of?" She cocked her head at him.

"Well, it's more than training dolphins," Bobby explained. "See, he's in business with a couple guys from down south around Texas or Louisiana. A seafood business. Shrimp. But it costs a lot of money to bring the shrimp up north because they've got to ship them in refrigerated trucks. The cost of that shipping was really killing the business."

"I'm sure," Miss Davenport said, nodding. She had huge blue eyes that never seemed to blink.

"So my father and friends came up with an idea. They would try to use dolphins to herd the shrimp up north!"

She gave him a quizzical look.

"And it worked!" Bobby thumped the desk. "Now they have three dozen trained dolphins that herd shrimp from the Gulf of Mexico right up the Gulf Stream. My father has a crew of boats that harvest the shrimp right off New Jersey. No trucks needed! That cuts out the middle man and allows Dad to sell the shrimp a lot cheaper than anyone else."

"Wait a sec," Miss Davenport said. "Let me get this straight. You're telling me that your father trains dolphins to herd shrimp from the Gulf of Mexico up to New Jersey? You're not pulling my leg, are you?"

"No, ma'am! It sounded crazy when he first thought of it, but it worked! The great thing is the shrimp never have to get frozen at all. And the shrimp they harvest are nice and plump from feeding in the Gulf Stream all the way north. You should taste them."

His stomach growled—all of a sudden those juicy shrimp really sounded delicious.

"Amazing," Miss Davenport said. She slowly shook her head and jotted something down on a piece of paper. "How does he do it? Train the dolphins, I mean."

"Dad had to hire a dolphin specialist for that,"

Bobby explained. He liked the sound of that: *dolphin specialist*. "I guess it took a lot of time. But after they trained one group of dolphins they discovered the most amazing thing. The female dolphins had babies, and after that Dad never had to train the babies—the parents taught their own babies how to herd the shrimp! You know how smart dolphins are. So now they don't even have to train them at all!"

Miss Davenport smiled and shook her head.

*

At the end of school, right after the final bell, Bobby saw Mom and Dad standing outside the main office. Dad was wearing a suit and tie; Mom had on her white nursing outfit. Neither one of them seemed happy to see him. Seeing your parents in school, he realized, almost always spells T-R-O-U-B-L-E.

"Hi," he said. "What's up?"

"Miss Davenport called," Mom said. "Your new guidance counselor. She asked us to come in for a talk."

"I think it's time we all go get an ice cream," Dad said.

"Somebody die?" Bobby muttered, following them out of the building. Mom and Dad took him out for ice cream whenever he got an A on a report card. Or when it was time to have a Serious Talk.

A strained silence inside the car. Mom swiveled her head around to look at him.

"How was your day?" she asked.

"Okay," he mumbled and that was it. Nobody said anything else until they arrived at Meg's Ice Cream Shoppe. They took a booth at the far end of the restaurant. As soon as the waitress took their order, Mom got up to use the rest room. Dad cleared his throat.

"I got a call from Miss Davenport," Dad said. "She said you told her an outlandish story today. About how I train porpoises to herd shrimp from the Gulf of Mexico up to New Jersey."

Bobby lowered his eyes to avoid his father's stare.

"That's the best one I've heard in a while," Dad said. "Well, she's a psychologist. She's trained to watch for stuff like this. So she did a little detective work, you know, talking to your other teachers. And it turns out you've been spreading around a bunch of different stories about your life. And about me. Let's see, you told one class that I run a silk farm. Spider silk. You told somebody else that I've just been named the head of the spider department at some big museum." Dad leaned back and folded his arms. "Maybe you'd like to tell me what *other* unusual jobs I have. Hmmm?"

Bobby sighed, looked away.

"Would you like to tell me what's going on?" Dad asked.

"I don't know," he mumbled.

"You don't know," Dad said, folding his arms. "Well, Miss Davenport is a little worried about you. She said it could be just a matter of adjusting to a new school. But she also used words like *closed off, unstable identity, at-risk adolescent*."

"Aw, c'mon," Bobby said. He lifted his spoon off the napkin and looked at his face, distorted, in the metal.

"Your mother's worried," Dad said. "All you seem to read and write about is spiders. She thinks you're a little obsessed with that tarantula of yours."

The voice in Bobby's head replied, *Right now Thelma's the best friend I've got*. He decided that it would not be smart to say this out loud. Definitely not.

"I don't know what to think of all these stories you've been telling about me," Dad was saying. "Amazing jobs. Inventor of this. Director of that. Trouble is, I don't have a job like that."

"I know, I know."

"I'm production manager at a container plant. We make cardboard boxes. And I'm not ashamed of that. It's a job. I get paid well. And it takes a lot of money to run a family."

Bobby sighed. He had heard the money lecture before, but he knew he couldn't stop it now. It was like a machine with a button that, once pushed, couldn't be stopped but had to run through until it was finished.

"All my adult life I've had this goal to earn my own age in salary. Well, I'm forty-three now, and for the first time in my life I'm doing that, plus a couple grand." Dad looked down at his hands. "It's not training dolphins or winning the Nobel Prize by studying the deadly three-headed vampire from Katmandu. But it's a good job with good benefits. And that's why we moved here."

"I know, I know," Bobby said. Mom returned just as the waitress showed up with their cones, each lying in its own small dish.

"Who gets the nonfat blueberry yogurt?" the waitress asked.

"I do," Mom said. She put the dish in front of her and didn't touch it.

"I'm worried," she said after the waitress left. At that moment Bobby noticed all the tiny lines, like the finest webs, around her eyes.

He sighed again. "But there's, like, nothing to worry about. I'm okay. Really."

"I worry that you're isolated from people," she said. "Nobody calls you."

"I've only been here a few weeks," Bobby said. "It takes time to make friends." That sounded like something you'd hear on TV. *It takes time to make friends*. He licked his ice cream. Heavy on the green dye, light on the pistachio nuts.

"I know it's been hard for you," Mom said in a soft voice. "Leaving all your friends behind."

"Yeah."

"We all miss Naperville," Mom said.

"Wish we'd never left," Bobby muttered, glancing at his watch. In Naperville it was exactly 3:00 P.M. The long final bell. Kids racing for the door and all that sweet outside air. Bobby squirmed. How much longer before he could make his own exit?

"Help me understand all these make-believe stories," Mom said.

"We were just talking about that," Dad said.

"The other day when the car broke down you told the mechanic a story that scared him near to death. That doesn't sound like the Bobby Ballenger I know. You were always interested in the truth about things. What's going on?"

"I don't know," Bobby said. All at once he was tired of their questioning. *Who knows why I did it? Who knows why people do anything?* "It's like, I was bored, kind of."

"And angry about having to move," Mom put in.

Bobby shrugged. He'd eaten his cone too fast. The ice cream had numbed his tongue and planted the seed of a headache in the front of his head.

"I don't know if we should be worried about you or not," Mom said. "Miss Davenport said that sometimes when adolescents start telling all

53

kinds of made-up stories it can be a warning sign. Like a cry for help."

"Not," Bobby said. "I've always liked to make up stuff."

Dad motioned to the waitress.

"Could we have some water, please?" He looked at Bobby. "I remember when you were five years old you wanted to be an astronaut. For a whole year it was nothing but space, spaceships, asteroids. You wanted to change your name to Astronaut and you cried when we couldn't find you an astronaut costume for Halloween."

Mom nodded.

"And in first grade you were a paleontologist," Dad said. "That year it was nothing but dinosaur books, dinosaur movies, dinosaur pictures. The meat eaters and the plant eaters. You were a pterodactyl for Halloween."

Mom nodded hopefully. The waitress set down three small glasses of ice water.

"I'm no psychologist," Dad said, shrugging. "But for me, that's what adolescence was about. Figuring out who I was. It's hard work. Maybe you're going through that now."

"Maybe," Bobby said, shifting in his seat.

"Are you all right?" Mom asked.

"Yes, I'm fine. Really. Can we go now?"

"Just one more thing," Dad said. "Don't you think you better go back and tell all those people the truth about those stories you've been telling?"

"Yeah, I guess so," Bobby said after a moment.

"Good," Dad said. "I'll let you decide how to do that."

"Okay," Bobby said uneasily. What a relief it was to get out of that place. It always made him nervous when his parents thought they had him all figured out.

Six

Spiders can use a strand of silk web like a balloon to float away. This is called gossamer flight.

No way a couple hundred baby spiderlings could find enough food to survive in one small area. Spiders had to invent some way of spreading out so they could find new places to hunt and live.

Gossamer flight just may be the most amazing thing spiders do. Here's how it happens:

Spiders like to "fly" on warm sunny mornings when there might be an updraft in the air. The little spider climbs to the top of the tallest object it can find. It stands on tiptoes and turns around to face the wind.

The spider squeezes out a little drop of silk from its spinnerets. This thread gets quickly hauled out by the wind and used like a sail. The wind lifts the thread. When the pull from the thread is strong enough the spider lets go and floats away.

Ballooning spiders have been found floating up to nine thousand feet in the air. Scientists have found that the stomachs of swallows contained lots of small black spiders.

Gossamer flight happens all around the world—in China, Brazil, Greece, and Australia. They float through the air and land on islands in the ocean. One explorer at the top of Mt. Everest found tiny jumping spiders at 22,000 feet!

In some places, the threads of the ballooning spiders get mixed together and whole sheets of gossamer (spider silk) rain down on fields, trees, the sides of mountains. I'd love to see that! Scientists used to think that the threads were all from the same species—the gossamer spider—but now they know that lots of spiders use their silk to travel by air.

Imagine it: the spider floats way up in the air, clinging to that strand of silk. Air currents are much stronger at high altitudes than they are on *the ground. Pretty soon the spider has flown hundreds of miles from home. What a trip!*

I'd love to balloon out of here.

I can picture myself doing it, floating back to Naperville, to our old stucco house on Locust Street. Wouldn't Mike and Chad and Cody be amazed to see me come parachuting down from the sky?

But spiders don't go ballooning for fun. They do it to survive. Most young spiders use this aerial flight at some time in their lives. But not big spiders like tarantulas. Even as a baby, a spider like Thelma would be way too heavy to balloon up into the air.

Thelma and I are in the same boat—both stuck in New Paltz, New York. We can't leave. Our only choice is to try to find a way to survive right here.

Bobby survived as best he could. At school he stood up and told Mr. Niezgocki's class the truth about his father's silk farm. He apologized to them, and he apologized separately to Mr. Niezgocki. He also apologized to Mrs. Nederhauser, Miss Terbaldi, and Miss Davenport for the stories he had told them.

The apologies were a lot easier than he'd imagined. *I'm sorry. I'm really sorry.* A few kids in Mr. Niezgocki's class gave him funny looks, and Chick Hall smirked, but most just shrugged it off.

He had thought that apologizing would make him feel better. Lighter. It didn't. Still, he decided he wouldn't tell any more stories. From now on he would concentrate on being Bobby Ballenger. No more lies.

*

That night after supper he got a phone call.

"Hi, could I speak to Bobby please?"

"That's me."

"This is Lucky Prescott. From Mr. Niezgocki's class?"

"Oh, yeah."

"I figured we better get cracking on that research project we're supposed to do together. I figured I'd better give you a call."

"Yeah, right."

"I was thinking maybe I should come over so we can work on it. It's due Monday, you know."

"When?" he asked, stalling. He had absolutely no interest in doing a research project with her, or any other total stranger.

"I don't know. Tomorrow afternoon sometime?"

"Hmmm," Bobby said. He couldn't see any way out of it.

"If we're going to do it, we might as well do it right," Lucky said. "We can do something about spiders if you want."

"What about spiders?"

"I don't know . . . you're the expert. Maybe something about poisonous spiders . . . ? My father's friend in Atlanta got bit by a brown recluse."

"No way. Really?"

"Yeah, he was cleaning out his attic," Lucky said. "Never saw the critter till it was too late. Boy, did he get sick! Twice they had to give him the last rites. He didn't die, but his face got all messed up—he had to have surgery to make him look sort of normal again."

Bobby swallowed. The brown recluse was probably the most dangerous spider living in the United States.

"How about I come over tomorrow after lunch? See if we can't get started on this thing. We could work over here, but I'm going out for a run anyway and I think I come near your house. You live on Sumac, right?"

"Yeah. First yellow house on the left."

"See you tomorrow?"

"All right," Bobby said. He hung up and let out a sigh.

"Who was that?" Bobby's father asked. He was sitting at the breakfast bar, thumbing through the newspaper.

"That was a girl in my class. Mr. Niezgocki put us together to work on a class project. She's going to come over tomorrow so we can work on it."

"That's nice," his mother said, smiling over at him.

"She's black," he added.

"Hmmm," his father said, nodding casually.

"When she's coming?" Mom asked.

"Tomorrow after lunch," he said. "And I'd really appreciate it if nobody made a big deal about it."

*

The next day Lucky showed up in a gray Atlanta Braves sweat suit with purple sweatbands on her wrists and forehead. Dad and Mom looked up from where they were working in the garden.

"Hi," Lucky said.

"Hello!" Mom replied.

"Hi!" Dad grinned, showing his dirty hands. "I'd shake hands but . . ."

"Isn't it kind of late to be planting?" Lucky asked.

"We're putting in iris bulbs for next spring," Mom explained. "They're from my garden back in Illinois. We brought a little bit of home with us."

They walked into the kitchen.

"So you're a runner," Mom said, washing her hands in the sink. "I run, too. How far do you go?"

"Somewhere around three miles," Lucky said. "Weekends I might do a little more. I'm going out for the cross-country team. Lucky for me I inherited my daddy's strong legs."

"I just broke three miles," Mom said. "I usually get up real early to run. Six, or six fifteen."

Bobby stood there, hands jammed in pockets. For a panicky moment he wondered if Mom and Lucky would set up a date to go running together.

"Wow," Lucky said. "No way I could run that early!"

"I figured you two might like something to nibble on," Mom said, setting down a plate of brownies and tall glasses of milk.

"You make these?" Lucky asked, leaning forward.

"Who me?" Mom asked. "No! My husband is the chef around here. I got these at a bakery near the hospital where I work."

Bobby sat down at the breakfast bar, glaring at his mother. He had asked her not to do anything special for this visit. But of course, she didn't listen. She never did. He picked up a brownie and nibbled on one corner. Lucky sat across the table from him.

"No way my ma would let my father into the kitchen to cook," Lucky said.

There was a sudden rumble on the stairs; Breezy poked her head into the room.

"Bobby," Mom said, "aren't you going to do the introductions?"

"My sister, Brianna," Bobby mumbled.

"Breezy," she corrected him, extending her hand.

"I'm Lucky," she said, shaking it.

"You are?" Breezy asked. She looked confused.

"I mean that's my name, Lucky," Lucky explained.

"Oh, Lucky's your *name*," Breezy said, smiling. "Hey, that's cool. Mmmm. Brownies."

"Don't you have play practice or something?" Bobby asked her.

"No rush," Breezy said sweetly. Ignoring his glare, she sat down, taking the seat directly across from Lucky.

"Have you lived here a long time?" Mom asked.

"No, ma'am," Lucky said. "We just moved here this summer, from Atlanta."

"Like us!" Mom said. "Bobby probably told you that we just moved here from Illinois. What do your parents do?"

"Mom's a nurse. She just took a job at Whispering Pines. It's a nursing home for people with Alzheimer's. My father's a news anchorman on TV. Roland Prescott."

"Roland Prescott!" Mom exclaimed. She and Breezy stared at each other. Lucky nodded, her mouth full of brownie.

"Channel eight, right?" Breezy beamed. "Hey, a celebrity!"

Bobby drummed his fingers on the table.

63

Exactly how long, he wondered, was this little interview going to last?

"Do you mind if I ask about your name?" Mom asked. "How is it people call you Lucky?"

"My real name is Amber," she replied. "But I've always hated that name. It seems *so* common."

Bobby finished the brownie. He had several nice chunks of amber in his rock collection. The stone weighed practically nothing. Amber was made from fossilized tree sap. In a piece of amber you could find tiny preserved insects from millions of years ago—flies, even small spiders.

"Lucky's a nickname. See, I was born on Friday the thirteenth, August thirteenth, at twelve thirteen in the morning. When I was born I weighed seven pounds, thirteen ounces. All those thirteens, and somehow everybody started calling me Lucky. And the name just stuck."

"Perfect!" Breezy exclaimed.

"It fits me," Lucky said. "Because I really am lucky. All the time I'm lucky. Today I found two quarters while I was running."

She opened her hand to show the coins.

"You mind holding them for me?" she asked Bobby. "My sweatpants don't have pockets."

Bobby took the two quarters and tucked them in the front pocket of his jeans.

"Hey, Bobby," Breezy said, "you going to introduce her to the family's fierce and diabolical killer?"

64

Lucky looked at him.

"Follow me," he said. They went up the stairs and into his room.

"Nice," Lucky said. "You could do a lot with this room. Lots of closet space, looks like. You plan on moving in?"

"Someday," Bobby said. Beyond the four quarter-circle windows there were two closets with built-in shelves. Right now they were full of old paint cans. He bent down and lifted the screen top off the terrarium. Thelma was in her usual position, lying behind a rock, scrunched up in the corner. Very gently he lifted her out. The spider nearly filled the space made by his cupped hands.

"Easy, girl," Bobby said. "This is Thelma. She's a tarantula."

"Man, man, man," Lucky whispered. She sat next to him on the bed and lowered her head to take a good look at Thelma. "Is that . . . safe?"

"Yeah," he said, softly touching the hair on Thelma's body. "The most she can do is give you a little nip. Doesn't even break the skin. Last summer when I first got her, I used to let her walk on my chest, but I got a little rash. From her hairs, I guess. So I don't do that anymore."

"Do tarantulas live around here?" Lucky asked.

"Tarantulas in New York?" Bobby laughed. "No! You won't find any tarantulas living in this part of the country. Thelma's from Chile, South America. A Chilean rose tarantula."

65

Lucky looked relieved. "Can I, ah, touch her?"

"Sure, go ahead."

Carefully she put the tip of her forefinger against one of Thelma's legs.

"She's real gentle," Bobby said.

"Where'd you get her?"

"My friends in Illinois gave her to me. She was sort of a goodbye present."

"So what does she eat?"

"She likes crickets," Bobby said. "But you can feed tarantulas other stuff, too."

"Like what?" she asked in a low voice.

"You really want to know?"

She nodded.

"Small mice."

She made a face at that.

"I don't feed her mice, but some people do," Bobby said. "Anyway, it doesn't seem to matter what I feed her these days. She hasn't been eating since we moved here."

"Maybe she's homesick. I've felt that way myself, off and on, since we drove up from Georgia. Thank God for my running. When I don't run, I get awful glum." She reached over and touched Thelma again. "Maybe she just needs a friend."

"Maybe," he said. He put Thelma back in the terrarium.

"Are you any good?" Bobby asked. "At running, I mean."

"Not bad. I bet I'm the fastest kid in the school."

"How do you know?"

She shrugged.

"Don't know, really. It's just that I've *always* been the fastest kid in school. My last school went up to sixth grade, and by the time I was in third grade nobody could beat me." She rubbed her belly. "I really shouldn't have eaten that brownie. I'm in training almost all the time. There's going to be another Olympics in six years, and I plan to be there."

That I'm-so-sure-of-myself tone irked him. It reminded him of Chick Hall. Maybe being a jock made you feel and act cocky like that. Or having a father on TV.

"So what about this project we're supposed to do?" she asked.

"C'mon outside," he said, getting up. "I want to show you something."

They went out back. The one thing he liked about the new house was how much room they had. There was a big lawn, a field of tall grass and wildflowers, and woods beyond that. Fifty feet into the field they came upon a little vegetable garden with rows of squash, pumpkins, and tomatoes.

"Here," Bobby said, motioning for her to stop at the edge of the garden. That's when Lucky saw them—spiders. Not as giant as Thelma, but big, plenty big. In the sunlight they were a brilliant yellow and black color, sitting at the hub of circular webs. In the breeze the webs billowed like little sails.

"Hey, wow, are they poisonous?" Lucky stammered.

"Nope, they're garden spiders. Totally harmless." To show her, he carefully lifted one of the spiders off its web. The spider didn't like this and tried to squirm away.

"Boy, you *are* an expert, aren't you?"

He shrugged and put the garden spider back in its web.

"Last summer I read this book about the Aborigines, in Australia," Lucky said. "It said sometimes the Aborigines do this thing where they take a big leaf and swipe at a spider web so they can collect the whole thing. It's funny. The Aborigines think of a spider's web as a piece of art. They decorate their houses with them."

Bobby nodded and made a mental note to check that fact. Exactly the sort of thing he might put in his spider journal.

They both sat down and started talking about the science project for Mr. Niezgocki's class. They decided to concentrate on poisonous spiders around the world. Lucky would make some illustrated diagrams. He would get a piece of poster board and make a list of unusual spider facts. He could do that in his sleep.

"I was thinking maybe I could bring in Thelma as part of our report," Bobby said as they walked back toward the house. "Mr. Niezgocki said it would be all right."

"Okay," Lucky said. When they reached the driveway she leaned forward and began to stretch. She leaned forward, knees locked, and put her whole hands on the ground. She stood up with her eyes closed and stretched her arms skyward. Deep breath. She opened her eyes and looked at him. And then without warning she was off, long legs moving sure and smooth and fluid as she ran up the driveway and onto the road.

"See ya!" she called. He stood watching as she rounded the bend. When he turned to walk into the house something jingled in his pocket.

"Hey!" he yelled. "You forgot your quarters!"

But he knew his words could never catch her.

Seven

October 4

I keep thinking about Lucky's father's friend who got bit by a brown recluse spider and nearly died. Twice a priest gave him the last rites. Extreme unction, they call it. When a brown recluse bites you, the skin dies around the wound. This guy's face got messed up so bad the doctors had to do plastic surgery to make it look semi-normal.

All spiders have some poison but in most spiders the poison is too weak to be a threat to humans. Still, you have to be careful. More people die every year from spider bites than from shark attacks.

One of the most dreaded and dangerous spiders

in South Africa is the button spider. Its poison is supposed to be four times as strong as a cobra's. When you get bit you feel burning at the bite. Then your chest and stomach muscles get paralyzed. You feel sharp pain and numbness in your left arm. Your pulse rate becomes quick. Pretty soon you're a goner.

The funnel spider (Australia) is also deadly. Last year a two year old boy died within an hour and a half of being bitten.

There is a spider in South Africa, the spitting spider (scientific name is Scydotes), that creeps up to its prey. When it gets close enough, it spits. The spit is sticky and has lots of poison in it. The gummy mass covers the spider's victim and pins it to the ground. The spitting spider moves forward slowly and gives the final bite. Then he drags the victim from the sticky mass and eats it. I guess if your poison is strong enough, it doesn't matter how fast or slow you are.

Bobby walked down the crowded halls at school and heard a strange sound: somebody whistling. With a start he realized it was his own whistling—a sound he hadn't heard once since he'd moved to New Paltz.

He was in a good mood. The oral presentation

he and Lucky did in Mr. Niezgocki's class went great, especially when he brought Thelma out for everyone in class to see. After one giant gasp—one girl actually had to leave the room—the whole class gathered around to meet Thelma up close. The kids really liked her.

He whistled his way into the lunchroom and found Lucky sitting at the table where he usually sat.

"Hi," she said. "You don't mind if I sit here, do you?"

"Nope." He opened his lunch bag—a meatloaf sandwich along with all the other things Dad had packed.

"Hey, I stopped by Mr. N's class and he gave me our grade," Lucky said. "A for content and A for presentation."

"Yesss!" Bobby said, making a fist.

"He said we had the whole class hooked."

"Not the whole class," Bobby said. "Chick Hall was absent."

"True. He's been hassling you, huh? Spider Boy and all that?"

"Every day I come into homeroom and find all these notes and signs on my desk. 'Dear Spider Boy.' 'Let's hear it for the world famous Spider Boy.' It's so stupid."

"Yeah, he's a little annoying," Lucky admitted. "But all in all, the guy is pretty harmless."

"Chick Hall?" He stopped chewing.

72

"He's not evil or anything." Lucky smiled at him. "I mean I know he's obnoxious sometimes, but who isn't? I sort of like him."

"You sort of like him?" He couldn't believe his ears.

"Yeah, well, at least he keeps things lively around here. Some days I feel like I'm going to die of boredom."

He glared at her. Lucky Prescott liked Chick Hall. This made no sense.

"Chick saved someone's life last summer," Lucky said.

"So big deal," he said. "I saved a kid's life myself, back in Illinois."

"Really?" She leaned forward and a story sprang to his lips. He was playing hockey, a sudden jagged crack in the ice, two little boys plunging into black water. . . . She would never doubt it. But it didn't feel right, not with Lucky. Besides, he'd made that resolution. No more lies.

"Nah," he said. "Just kidding."

"Bobby Ballenger!" She gave him a pouty look. "You had me going, you fiend! Hey, you know Thelma looked great today. You get her a perm for the occasion?"

"Very funny."

"Does she get an extra-juicy cricket for being good?"

"She gets all the crickets she wants, but she's not eating anything." He dropped the half-eaten meatloaf sandwich into his lunch bag. The talk about Chick had killed his appetite.

"She won't starve," Lucky said. "Least that's what my grandma used to say when my little brother didn't want supper. Where's Thelma now?"

"Mr. Niezgocki's letting me keep her in his lab."

"So you can stop in and see her whenever you want, huh? That's pretty cozy." She raised her eyebrows. "You know, that would make some girls jealous. See ya."

She picked up her lunch tray and walked away.

*

Back home, Bobby walked in and found his father sitting in the kitchen with a big smile on his face.

"Hi, Dad." Bobby stopped. "What're you doing home so early?"

"I've got a surprise for you."

"What?"

"Go up to your bedroom."

Bobby dropped his knapsack and ran upstairs, taking the steps two at a time. Everything looked normal in his room: the bed in the corner, the walls that needed painting, the stack of rolled-up posters, and boxes of unpacked books. Bobby glanced at the big terrarium where Thelma lived. Then he remembered that he had taken Thelma and her terrarium to school and left her there.

"Thelma?" he asked, peering inside.

"Observe carefully, Mr. Scientist," Dad said, coming into the room.

There was a tarantula inside the terrarium, but it wasn't Thelma. This one was bigger. Its legs and body were covered by short, fine hairs that were a dark reddish color.

"What is it?" Bobby sputtered.

"You are looking at a male king baboon spider." Dad spoke the words slowly. "An African baboon spider. Happy birthday!"

"What . . . I mean how—?"

"I hadn't planned on getting you another spider, but a few days ago I started talking to a guy at work. His son had this tarantula for about a year. The kid went off to college and his father didn't want to take care of him. He was going to sell it back to the pet store but asked me if I was interested. These tarantulas can be pretty expensive, but the guy gave me a great price. Plus he threw in the tank and all this equipment for free. What do you think? Like him?"

"I love him!" Bobby said. "Can I hold him?"

"No!" Dad said, holding up both hands. "The guy at work said baboon spiders can deliver a serious bite. He gave me these gloves to wear if you have to reach into the tank."

Bobby put them on. They were made of rubber and reached all the way up to his elbows.

"Do you have anything to feed him?" Dad asked.

"I think so," Bobby said, looking into the card-board box where he kept the crickets. He lifted the hood and carefully dropped in a live cricket. The insect had barely landed on the sand when the spider came racing over, pounced, and bit it savagely. Even at her hungriest, Thelma had never been so ferocious.

"I *guess* he's hungry!" Dad said. "You'd better make sure you've got enough!"

Bobby sat there, watching the tarantula feast. It had been such a long time since he'd seen Thelma eat anything at all.

"Are you going to name him?" Dad asked.

"Hmmm," Bobby said as his mind made a chain in rapid speed: baboon spider, baboon, monkey, monk.

Monk.

*

Dad made chicken paprikash for dinner. Mom switched on the TV so they could watch Roland Prescott do the news. He was a tall man with glasses and a short-cropped beard. Bobby thought the man looked like a professor.

"Hey, your girlfriend's father," Breezy said.

"Not a girlfriend," Bobby said. "Barely a friend."

"Don't be so testy," Breezy said, helping herself to the salad. "I liked her. She's nice—and real pretty. That girl's hot. A definite fox."

"Lucky is an attractive girl," Dad agreed.

76

"Attractive?" Breezy snorted. "I'd say beautiful is a lot closer to it. On a scale of one to ten, I'd give her at least an eight. Maybe a nine."

"Oh, and I suppose you're a ten," Bobby said.

"Don't I wish." Breezy sighed. "No, I figure on a real good day I might be a seven, possibly a seven and a half."

"In my book you're a ten all the way," Dad said, leaning toward Breezy so she could plant a kiss on his cheek.

"You *sure* she's not your girlfriend?" Breezy teased. "You're awful quiet over there."

"If I ever have a girlfriend I promise you'll be the first to know," Bobby told her.

"Well, *I'm* not shy about my boyfriend," Breezy said. "Luke has taken me on two dates now. He's really, really nice. And he's a *phenomenal* swimmer, one of the best in the state."

"Luke?" Bobby got a sudden fluttery sensation in the pit of his stomach. "What's his last name?"

"Hall. Can I have the dressing, please?"

Bobby let his head fall into his hands. Luke Hall! His sister was going out with Chick Hall's big brother! Mr. Webbed Feet. Mr. All-American-Full-Scholarship-to-Yale! He stared at the TV. Roland Prescott's face had turned serious, two people killed in a wreck on the interstate.

"What's wrong with you?" Breezy asked him.

"Luke Hall's brother, Chick, is in my class, and he's the biggest pain-in-the-you-know-what in the whole school." Bobby moaned. "Of all the kids in the high school, why'd you have to pick *him* to go out with?"

"Maybe he's different," Mom said.

"Yeah," Bobby replied. "And maybe we'll move back to Naperville tomorrow and forget New Paltz ever existed."

"Oh, I am so terribly sorry, dearest brother," Breezy said, pressing her palms together as if in prayer. "Next time I'll be sure to clear all my dates with you ahead of time, all right? Okay?"

"This is the one time we sit down together as a family," Dad said. He reached over and turned off the TV. "Let's try not to scratch each other's eyes out."

"Mom, could Luke come over for dinner sometime? I'd like him to meet you guys."

Dad and Mom exchanged looks.

"I don't see why not," Mom said.

"Maybe tomorrow?" Breezy asked. "I wanted him to come over Saturday, but he's got a big swim meet that night. It doesn't have to be fancy or anything."

The phone rang.

"That might be him now," Breezy said, jumping up. But after saying hello, she covered the receiver and pointed at Bobby.

"Does your girlfriend have a deep voice?"

Bobby grabbed the phone and walked around to the other side of the breakfast bar.

"Hi," the voice said. "It's Lucky."

"Oh, hi." Bobby ignored Breezy, who was making eyes at him.

"Everything okay?"

"Yeah. Sure. We're watching your dad on TV."

"You sure don't seem too happy about it."

"It's not him," Bobby said in a quiet voice. "It's, you know, family stuff."

"Oh." For almost ten seconds, neither of them said anything. She cleared her throat.

"Well, I was wondering if you wanted to come over this Saturday night," Lucky said. "My dad just got a new telescope. He's a real astronomy nut. Saturday's supposed to be clear. We should be able to get a good view of Saturn."

Bobby stood there watching his sister watch him.

"Uh-huh." He cleared his throat. "Well, um, I don't think so. See, I'm sort of busy this weekend."

"Oh, okay." Another pause. "Okay. Maybe some other time."

"Yeah, sure."

"See you tomorrow."

"Okay. Bye."

*

After supper he went upstairs. His room was quiet. He peered into the terrarium and saw Monk, almost motionless, still sucking the juice out of his cricket.

Bobby took out a magnifying glass and looked down at the tarantula. He put the glass directly over the spider's face and saw Monk looking up at him. A face alert, curious, somehow intelligent. A creature so incredibly ugly he was beautiful.

Eight

October 5

The guy who sold Monk to Dad gave him a book on how to take care of tarantulas—Arachnomania by Philippe de Vosjoli. It has tons of great stuff about the African king baboon spider and other kinds of tarantulas, too.

There are about 800 different tarantula species in the world.

The king baboon spider is the second largest African tarantula. They are big and beautiful, covered with short red hairs. Females are bigger than the males. That's true of all tarantulas.

King baboons are considered aggressive tarantulas. These little monsters come at you hissing,

with their fangs raised. Dad was right: You defi-
nitely don't want to handle this species.

Tarantulas are "primitive" spiders—living fossils.
They haven't changed much through evolution
from the way they were tens of millions of years
ago. No fancy webs for these creatures. They get
their food the old-fashioned way by overpowering
their prey with strength, speed, and viciousness.
Earth tigers.

Adult tarantulas eat crickets, mealworms, and
small pink mice. (Why pink, I wonder?) Spider-
lings can eat pinhead crickets or wingless fruit-
flies until they get bigger.

Young tarantulas should be offered food twice a
week. Adult spiders can be offered food every
week to ten days. If you get a tarantula that's
been imported from another country and it has a
shrunken abdomen, that usually means it hasn't
been eating enough. They should be fed more fre-
quently.

The book has lots of helpful information, but
some of the author's advice is really funny even
though he probably didn't mean it to be:

Young children should not be allowed to handle
tarantulas. (Gee, really?)

If you're going to hold a tarantula, sit on the rug, or a soft couch. The biggest risk of handling tarantulas is that they'll fall and split open their abdomens when they hit the ground. The tarantulas usually die when that happens but a few people have had some luck using a fast-drying glue to hold the split edges together. The author recommends Krazy Glue as a last resort to glue the tarantula back together!

Tarantula hairs can fall off and cause severe itching and allergic reactions in some people. Getting tarantula hairs in your eyes or mouth is no fun. Do not let them climb on your face.

Okay, I won't.

It's important to use common sense when taking care of large spiders. Tarantulas from the desert like their cage or terrarium kept hot. Tarantulas from tropical climates like it moist and humid. Tarantulas that climb trees need something to climb to feel like they're at home.

Think spider.

Suddenly Bobby heard a strange sound, a soft hissing coming from the terrarium, from Monk. He bent down to take a closer look. He had read about this sound some adult tarantulas make: *stridulation*. Even the word sounded dangerous.

Maybe Monk was still hungry. He opened the screen top and dropped in a live cricket. The baboon spider pounced in a blur of motion, pierced the insect with its sharp fangs, and sat motionless, sucking out the cricket's insides.

Bobby watched, fascinated. Even in her healthy days Thelma never ate like that. He thought about Thelma alone in Mr. Niezgocki's laboratory at school. All at once he missed the way she felt resting contentedly in the palm of his hand. How was she doing? Did she miss him?

Watching Monk eat, Bobby's own stomach gave a rumble. But then he remembered, *Luke Hall is coming to dinner tonight*. The thought started a sickly feeling in the pit of his stomach and erased whatever feeble appetite he might have had.

Fifteen minutes later Bobby flopped down at the breakfast bar and poured himself a small bowl of cornflakes.

"Morning," Mom said, smiling over at him from the ironing board. She was ironing her nurse's uniform.

"Where's Dad?" he asked.

"He's already up and out," Mom answered. "And I've got to get out, too. One of the nurses called in sick at the hospital."

"So how come you're in such a good mood?" Breezy said from her seat at the far end of the breakfast bar.

"Guess who's going to be in Maternity today?" Mom said, smiling. "Guess who gets to kiss all those brand-new babies? Moi!"

"Hey, Mom, what should we have for dinner tonight?"

"How about that four-alarm chili Dad makes?" Mom suggested. "That's always a big hit. We can make some corn bread to go with it."

"Luke doesn't like spicy food," Breezy said.

"Luke doesn't like spicy food," Bobby repeated in a nasal voice.

"Maybe he could make that nice shrimp dish," Mom said. "Shrimp over puff pastry."

"Great," Breezy said. She gave Bobby a sly grin. "I'll buy the shrimp. You know, I heard about this local shrimp herder who has the freshest, most wonderful shrimp you can imagine. You would not believe how he does it. See, he's got these porpoises, these trained dolphins who actually herd the shrimp up the East Coast—"

"Mom!" Bobby cried, dropping his spoon into the bowl. "How does . . . I mean . . . man! Doesn't the word 'privacy' mean *anything* around here?"

"I swear I'm innocent," Mom replied, lifting her hands.

Bobby finished his cereal. *Dad.*

"Relax, both of you."

"Why don't *you* cook, Brianna?" Bobby suggested.

"Oh no you don't," Breezy said. Luxuriously, she tossed her long hair. "I take after my very modern mother. I don't do windows and I don't cook. Except breakfast."

"You could at least make dessert," Bobby said. "Remember that jam cake you made last summer, the one that tasted like stale glue? That would impress any swimmer."

"Hold it, you two," his mother said. She put down the iron and approached the breakfast bar. "Hold it right there. I want you to be on your best manners tonight. Understand?"

"Truce?" Breezy looked at him.

"Oh, all right."

"You know, your watch is wrong," she said. "The clock in your room, too. They're off by an hour. You're an hour behind the rest of the world."

"Yeah, well it's, like, an experiment we're doing in my science class," Bobby lied. "Half the class switched to daylight savings time, half didn't."

"Whatever," Breezy sighed.

*

At school Bobby waded through the crowd of

kids drifting toward homeroom, thinking how terrific it would be if Chick Hall were absent for a whole week. A solid month.

"Spider Boy!"

Chick Hall stood before him, black hair wet and gleaming, flanked by two boys on one side, one on the other. *I swam a mile this morning,* his cocky smile seemed to say. *What have you done with* your *morning?*

"Missed you yesterday, Spider Boy!" Chick said, smirking. His front teeth were big and white. "I hear you brought your little brother to school yesterday! I woulda loved to meet the furry little beast!"

Bobby started pushing past but one of Chick's friends stepped in front of him and blocked the way. It was Scott Shanahan, a short, wiry boy with curly brown hair. Bobby had heard from Butch Fostick that Scott's father, Bird Shanahan, was a local garbage collector, a man of legendary physical strength.

"You know, I got a boa constrictor that'll make lunch meat out of your tarantula any day of the week," Scott said.

"Congratulations," Bobby said, shrugging and walking away.

"See ya in homeroom, Spider Boy!" Chick yelled. Bobby walked down the corridor to the sounds of a spirited chorus:

Spider boy! Spider boy!
Spider boy from Illinois!
He's the best in the West
Friend to all those spider pests—
Oh yeah! Here comes Spider Boy!
Oh yeah! Here comes Spider Boy!

Bobby slid into Mr. Niezgocki's lab and pulled the door shut behind him. He was surprised to find Lucky there.

"Hi," she said.

"Hi," he replied. Standing next to her, he was struck again at how tall she was. He was tall for his age, but she was every inch as tall as he was. Maybe an inch taller.

"Just came in to see how she's doing," Lucky said.

Thelma barely moved when Bobby lifted her out. The live cricket he'd given her for dinner was still jumping around. He sat down on the floor and put her on his lap. Thelma took two lazy steps up the front of his shirt. Then stopped.

"How are you, girl?" Bobby asked in a quiet voice. "You like it here okay? Huh?"

"She okay?" Lucky asked, sitting beside him.

"I guess so," Bobby said. "Still not eating. I've read that sometimes they go through a period where they don't eat for weeks, even months. It could be lots of reasons."

"Let me hold her?" Lucky asked softly. He looked at her.

"Okay, but be careful. Promise you won't freak out and drop her?"

"I promise, I promise."

"Be real careful. Cup your hands—just let her sit on your palms. Don't squeeze at all."

He placed Thelma in Lucky's hands. Thelma swiveled around, moving her furry feet until she found a comfortable position.

"She seems to like your smell all right," Bobby said. Eyes wide, Lucky grinned.

"She's heavy!" she whispered. "And the hairs are stiffer than I'd thought. Here."

She handed Thelma back to him.

"Can she see me? How do you think I look to her?"

"Blurry, probably," Bobby said. "These spiders have eight eyes, but they don't have very good eyesight for things far away. Whatever they can see is right up close."

He put Thelma back in her cage.

"Thanks for inviting me over this weekend," he said without looking at her. "I, uh, didn't exactly tell you the truth. I really don't have anything planned this weekend except that my sister is having Chick Hall's big brother over for dinner tonight. She's going out with him."

"Your big sister is going out with Chick's big

89

brother?" Lucky clapped her hands and spun around, laughing. "And he's coming to dinner? That's too perfect! I'd love to be a fly on the wall at your house tonight!"

"Yeah, I can't wait," Bobby said glumly. "Maybe that's why I'm a little down. It's like I'm having a bad—"

"Month?" Lucky put in.

"Yeah," he said with a short laugh.

"Well, the invitation's still open," she said. "If you change your mind, give me a call."

*

The bell rang in homeroom. Miss Terbaldi started taking attendance; two minutes later, Chick Hall came into the classroom.

"Mr. Hall," Miss Terbaldi said, frowning.

"I'm early," Chick said. "For first period."

Out of the corner of his eye, Bobby saw Lucky smile.

"Next time, Mr. Hall, don't bother coming without a late pass from the office."

"Yes, ma'am," Chick said.

On the way out of class, Chick slapped Lucky's arm.

"Hey!" she cried, a mixture of anger and delight on her face. She whirled around and smacked Chick back.

Later he saw them talking together in the hallway. They were both stretching, two athletes talking shop. Lucky had a bemused half-smile on her face. For guys like Chick, Bobby realized, life would always be good. Chick would always have nice cars, lots of money. Pretty girls.

In math class, Mr. Niezgocki droned on and on about the associative principle of mathematics. If $A = B$ and $B = C$, then $A = C$. A no-brainer. But even if this principle was true for A, B, and C, Bobby could see how worthless it was with people. He liked Lucky. Lucky liked Chick. Logically, he and Chick should be bosom buddies.

Yeah, right.

After school Bobby stopped into the lab to do his hour of work. It was fun being able to work so close to Thelma. He watered and misted Mr. Niezgocki's plants, fed the fish, and cleaned out the gecko's terrarium. Twice he reached into Thelma's terrarium to softly stroke her or whisper to her, just to let her know that he was there. Next he started working on the dissecting sets. He counted forty of them, most of them messed up, the scalpels and forceps put back the wrong way. He had about half of them done when Mr. Niezgocki arrived.

"Here," he said, handing back Bobby's spider journal. "Great stuff! I really enjoyed it."

"Really?"

"Yes, sir. Your love of spiders comes through

loud and clear. Not many people could see beauty in a spider, but you do. You see it, and you help me see it."

"Thanks." He felt pleased. "Mom's a little worried that I'm becoming obsessed."

"Obsessed?" Mr. Niezgocki shrugged. "What's wrong with being obsessed? Galileo, Einstein, Curie—obsessed, all of them. You tell your mom I said there's nothing wrong with that so long as you still leave time to be a human being."

"Okay," Bobby said.

"Can I make one suggestion?" Mr. Niezgocki asked. "The tidbits you've collected about spiders are fascinating, delicious, but my favorite parts of your journal were the parts about *you*, what you noticed, what you were thinking. You've got the eye and the heart of a scientist. Trust your perceptions and intuitions."

Bobby nodded.

"Now. Do you have a strong stomach?"

"I guess so," Bobby said.

"Then let me show you something you've probably never seen before."

He opened the refrigerator, took out a clear plastic bag, and held it up. That's when Bobby saw them. Eyes.

A whole bag of eyeballs. And he could tell in a split second that they were real, living eyes. Or had been living. He couldn't believe it. There must have been close to a hundred of them. It was like a scene from a horror movie: dead eyeballs, all looking at him blankly through the clear plastic.

"What the—"

"Pigs' eyes," Mr. Niezgocki said, grinning. "We're going to dissect them in science class, probably in early November."

"They look so . . ."

"Human?" Mr. Niezgocki nodded. "Sometimes they give us a shipment of sheeps' eyes. Those are really eerie. I've also gotten a shipment of cows' eyes, which are enormous. One of the advantages of working here is you get first crack at all this wonderful science stuff that comes in. Wait till we get the owl pellets." He smiled. "Say, would you like to take a few of these eyes home to study them?"

"Take them home? Could I?"

"Just promise to bring them back tomorrow."

"Promise," Bobby said.

*

Bobby walked home. There was a strange car parked in the driveway. A smug little Corvette, powder blue with a custom paint job, orange flames on both doors. Luke Hall's wheels.

Everyone was sitting in the living room. A plate of cheese and crackers on the coffee table. There was even one of those plastic logs burning in the fireplace. Luke was getting the red carpet treatment.

"The prodigal son returns," Breezy said, pointing at him. "That's Bobby."

"Hi," Bobby said with a short wave. He hoped Luke wouldn't get up off the couch, and he didn't.

"Hiya," Luke said. He was taller than Chick, with wider shoulders, but you could tell in a heartbeat that he and Chick were brothers. The same square jaw, slicked-back black hair. The same cocky smile.

"But like I was saying," Luke said, "the great thing about swimming is that you don't get the kind of injuries other athletes get, because the resistance gets spread out evenly on all the muscles in your body."

"Excuse me," Dad said, getting up. "I'd better check on dinner. Bobby, can you give me a hand?"

Gratefully, Bobby followed him into the kitchen.

"How was your day?" Dad asked.

"Okay," he said, but he could tell Dad wasn't listening; he was too intent on studying a pot of cooking shrimp.

"This is just about done. Be a sport and set the table for me? Forks, knives, spoons. Use cloth napkins, the red ones. In the fridge there's a bowl of pickles. And olives. Luke's crazy about green olives."

Luke's crazy about green olives. He could hear Luke in the living room talking about a conditioning program he did last summer at Yale.

94

"Doesn't all that lap swimming get repetitive?" Mom asked.

"No," Luke said. "Actually I find it clears my head."

Actually, Bobby thought, *I haven't heard such a pile of manure in a long, long time*. Bobby put the bowl of olives on the table. The large green olives reminded him of what he had tucked in his knapsack. Mr. Niezgocki had given him six pig eyes. He realized he'd better get them refrigerated.

He brought his knapsack into the dining room and took out the plastic bag. The eyeballs stared up at him. "There's a definite Zen to swimming," Luke was saying. "The mental part is ten times more important than the physical part."

Bobby took all six pig eyes out of the bag and added them to the bowl of olives. He arranged them carefully, making sure each eyeball was looking straight up. Then he buried the pig eyes beneath one layer of olives so they weren't visible from above.

"Okay," Bobby said when he finished.

"Table set?" Dad asked.

"Yeah," he replied. *It's set, all right*.

"Okay. We're going to eat in about ten minutes."

Bobby went upstairs. His heart was racing. To calm down he lay on the floor and took five deep breaths. He peered into the terrarium. Monk was lying motionless in a shallow burrow he'd dug at one end. *Most of a spider's life is spent waiting*.

Bobby waited. Seeing Monk made him think about Thelma. It occurred to him that when he left school he hadn't even thought to say goodbye.

"AAAHHH!"

The sound came from downstairs. Breezy's scream. This was followed by a confusion of shouting, scraping chairs, loud talking. A deep angry voice.

"Bobby! Come down here this instant!"

He walked down. His father was waiting for him on the landing. He grabbed Bobby's arm and escorted him into the dining room. Mom, Breezy, and Luke all stared at him.

"What is the meaning of this?" Dad asked, pointing at the bowl of olives. The top layer of olives was gone now; all you could see were the pig eyes. Staring up.

Bobby shrugged.

"Do those belong to you?" Dad asked. "Where did you get them?"

"They're pig eyes," Bobby said. "From my science teacher."

"What on earth are they doing in with the olives?" he demanded.

"I, uh, I, I . . ." Bobby stammered. What could he say?

"Eye is about right!" Luke said, starting to laugh.

That cracked the tension a tiny bit. Breezy looked at Luke, smiling uncertainly.

"It was, like, a practical joke," Bobby said, shrugging.

"Don't you have something to say?" Mom asked.

"Sorry?" Bobby offered, more of a question than anything else.

"Please, Bobby," Mom hissed. "Take those . . . things . . . out of here so we can eat!"

Bobby brought the bowl into the kitchen. He fished out the eyeballs and put them into a Ziploc plastic bag. Mom came in to get the pepper mill.

"I don't know what's gotten into you," she whispered tersely, "but I don't want any more nonsense. Right now I want you to wash your hands and come to dinner."

By the time Bobby returned, everyone had sat down. He took the last remaining seat next to Luke.

"Does this happen to all your guests?" Luke asked Breezy in a teasing voice.

"Told you I had a happy, normal family," Breezy replied with a big forced smile.

"Well," Mom said. "Shall we eat?"

"I vote *aye!*" Luke said with a short laugh. "And I think we'd have to agree that on this vote, the *eyes* have it!"

Breezy stared at Bobby and mouthed the words, *I'm gonna kill you.*

Nine

October 9

Got my newsletter today from the Tarantula Society of America. The big story was about some guy arrested for smuggling tarantulas from Mexico. They caught him with 600 spiders he bought for 3 dollars each in Mexico. He planned to sell them in the U.S. for 45 dollars each. They found the tarantulas all crowded together. Most of them were dehydrated. Some were missing legs. Some were dead.

People who would try to make a profit on endangered animals are about the lowest scum on earth. This idiot could get up to 25 years in jail and fines of over a million dollars. That's not enough, if you ask me.

Maybe someday I'll work for the government, helping to enforce the Endangered Species Act.

Mr. Niezgocki liked my spider journal. He's the first person I ever let read it. He wants me to put more stuff in about me. That doesn't sound very scientific, but I told him I'd think about it.

Took some pictures of Monk today. I'll take some pix of Thelma in school and send them to Mike and the guys.

Monk's an AWESOME tarantula. I wish Thelma had some of Monk's spunk. A couple of days ago I brought him downstairs. I put on the rubber gloves and sat with him on the floor but he jumped out of my hands and started running away. It was hilarious—he was running toward the living room and tried to swerve left around a corner, but his feet couldn't get any traction on the waxed floors. He slid about five feet. I could not stop laughing. Then Mom came in and told me to take him back upstairs before Brianna saw him and had a conniption.

One thing I notice about Brianna—she's a joiner. She got a lead part in West Side Story. She's hoping to join the Glee Club. She's going out for cheerleader. She's always doing stuff with her *boyfriend. She can't be alone. She's got to be with people every moment of her life.*

Not me.

Spiders don't need to be busy every moment of the day. Spiders are patient. Most of their life is spent waiting.

Many insects and other animals have to band together for protection: bees, ants, ducks, chickens, cows, and sheep. Herd animals can't think or stand up for themselves. They can't survive unless they're part of a group.

A spider doesn't waste time worrying about cooperating or working together. Alone, he spins his web at dawn. Alone, he sends up a silky sail and lets the wind send him off to some unknown world. No need for anybody else. No need to depend on the herd for food or protection. Spiders are loners. They survive through their own strength, their own skill, their own guts.

Sounds good to me.

On Saturday Butch Fostick called and asked if Bobby wanted to go to the mall. Reluctantly, he agreed. He didn't much like malls or shopping but he had nothing better to do.

Bobby was surprised to see the mall crowded on such a nice fall day. In Naperville on a day like this he and Mike and the guys would play football at Mike's house. He and Mike always ended up on the same team. Mike was skinny but he had a great arm. Mike played quarterback; Bobby played wide receiver.

"Go long," Mike would tell him. "I'll get the ball to you."

Bobby would sprint down the field and look up. Like magic the ball would be there, spinning, hanging like a ripe piece of fruit. All he had to do was reach up and pluck it from the sky. He wondered, *What lucky kid is catching one of Mike's perfect passes right now?*

"I want to go to the Hobby Shop," Butch said. "Need a new chess clock."

"Hey, you like football?" Bobby asked.

Butch shrugged. "Football's a lot like chess. Every player has certain things they can and can't do. Everybody has to work together to help the team."

"So you like it?"

"Hate it," Butch admitted. "Why would a little guy like me like getting stomped on by a bunch of gorillas? I go for games where strategy is more important than muscle. You ought to let me teach you how to play chess."

101

"I like contact sports," Bobby said. "Like football."

"If you don't think chess is a contact sport," Butch said, "you don't know the first thing about it."

Inside the Hobby Shop there was a large sign that read:

> THIS STORE USES ADVANCED
> ELECTRONIC SURVEILLANCE.
> ALL SHOPLIFTERS WILL BE
> PROSECUTED TO THE FULLEST
> EXTENT OF THE LAW.

"No honor system around here," Butch said, pointing at the sign.

"Huh?"

"The new honor system," Butch said. "They're starting it at school next week, and it's going to be real weird. Teachers can walk out of the room during a test. It'll be up to us kids to squeal if we see anybody cheating. I think it's a bad idea. I've got a theory about stuff like this. You want to hear it?"

"Do I have a choice?"

"My theory is people are basically evil," Butch said. "If people can cheat and get away with it, they will. The new honor system will last about three weeks. Remember, you heard it from me first."

They cruised through three more stores: Record World, Book-O-Rama, and Pets Galore (no tarantulas). Then they each bought a couple slices of pizza at the food court before Butch called his mother to come pick them up.

Back home the house seemed even quieter than before. Dad, Mom, and Breezy had gone to see a play and wouldn't be back until supper. Bobby wrote three short letters to Mike, Cody, and Chad. Then he lay on his bed, pitching his football up into the air. At 3:30 he flipped out of bed and picked up the phone. He dialed Mike's number and let the phone ring fifteen times before he finally hung up.

At around four o'clock he went downstairs and plopped down in front of the TV. He started watching a football game and reading a magazine article ("Lies People Believe About Spiders") all at the same time. The house stayed quiet as a morgue. A little later he went upstairs to check on Monk, who was resting quietly in his burrow after gorging himself on another live cricket.

At five o'clock Bobby took out his math folder and started studying for Monday's test. There were eight ditto pages of algebra problems. He yawned and tried to concentrate. At around five thirty he drifted over to the phone and picked it up. He'd only called Lucky a couple times, so he was surprised to discover he knew her number by heart.

"Hello?" He recognized Lucky's voice.

"Hi," he said. "It's Bobby."

103

"Hi." She sounded happy and a little surprised.

"Hi," he said stupidly. How many times would they say it?

"Just got back from a run," Lucky said.

"Yeah?" He tried to picture her, standing in her sweat suit, maybe, with a pink sweatband across her forehead. "I've been studying for the algebra test. They should use this stuff as sleeping pills. Five minutes and I'm, like, falling asleep."

"I know, I studied this morning. Hey, you never told me how dinner with Luke Hall went."

"It was fantastic." Bobby told her the whole story. When he got to the part about putting the pig eyes in with the green olives, Lucky started laughing and couldn't stop.

"Tell me you're making this story up," she managed. "Tell me!"

"No, it's true."

"You wicked thing!" She let out another peal of laughter. "Say, you still nursing that bad mood?"

"Not so much."

"Why don't you come over later? It's gonna be a real clear night."

"Well, yeah, I guess I can. I mean, I don't think I've ever looked through a real telescope before."

"Come at seven thirty if you can. Gets dark by then. Can you get a ride?"

"Yeah," he said. "No problem."

"Bring a jacket. We're going to be outside."

*

"It was nice of Lucky to invite you over," Mom said on the short ride to the Prescotts' house.

"Yeah."

"I'm glad you've found a friend."

"Yeah." He was glad she had not said *girlfriend*.

"She seems smart and sensible. And I do think she's striking. There it is! Bantam Street. Last house on the left."

She peered through the windshield and pulled the car over to the curb. "This must be the place. Have fun. Call me if you need a ride home, okay?"

Just as Bobby started getting out of the car the front door to the house opened, and none other than Roland Prescott, local TV anchorman, came out. Mom shot out of the car.

"Hello!" the man called. Bobby saw Lucky come out of the house behind him. For a moment everyone was smiling and shaking hands.

"You must be Bobby. And you must be Bobby's mother. I'm Roland Prescott." He had a deep, stirring voice. "My wife is inside. She's had a long day at work."

"You don't have to tell me, I'm a nurse myself," Mom said. "You know, we've seen you on TV. You're wonderful. We watch you all the time."

"Well, thank you," he said. "You're very kind. Won't you come in?"

105

Please, no, Bobby thought, and for once Mom read the situation right.

"Thank you, but I think I'll pass," she said. "My husband and I are going to enjoy a rare night in the house, all by ourselves. We're going to watch a movie."

"Well, we'll be watching a movie, too," Mr. Prescott said. He rubbed his beard and pointed up at the sky. "There's nothing like it."

"Looks like a perfect night," Mom said. "I'm sure it'll be breathtaking."

That word—*breathtaking*—sounded funny out there on the Prescotts' driveway. *Don't try so hard, Mom.* Bobby was relieved when she finally got back into the car and left.

He followed Lucky into the house, where he heard music. At the far end of the living room he saw a woman playing the piano.

"That's Ma," Lucky said. "Ma, this is Bobby. From school."

The woman rose from the piano and extended her hand to him.

"Hello, Bobby," she said. She had a nice smile. "I'm glad to meet you."

"Hi," Bobby said, taking her hand.

"That piece sounded good, Ma," Lucky said. "Really."

"Thanks, Lucky." Mrs. Prescott gave Bobby another smile. "This is the best part of my day."

"Hey, we going to use the telescope or what?"

Bobby turned in the direction of the voice and saw a boy, maybe eight, sitting on the couch and flipping through a pile of books.

"That's my brother, Sam," Lucky said to Bobby.

"Hi," Bobby said. Just then Mr. Prescott came into the room.

"I think we're just about ready," he said, putting his hand on Mrs. Prescott's shoulder. "Lila, are you going to join us?"

"No, I think I'll stay down here and enjoy this music," Mrs. Prescott replied. "You all have fun."

Everyone else followed Mr. Prescott upstairs and into a large room with a king-size bed. With some embarrassment Bobby realized they were walking through Mr. and Mrs. Prescott's bedroom. Mr. Prescott opened the door so they could all step outside onto a deck.

And there it was: the telescope, sleek and black, pointing skyward like a small cannon.

"I've been wanting one of these for years," Mr. Prescott said, rubbing his hands together. "Gave my family all kinds of hints around my birthday and Father's Day. Nothing. So, finally I went out and bought it myself."

"Dad, can I see first?" Sam asked, jumping on his tiptoes. "I'm gonna look for UFOs."

"Hold your horses," Mr. Prescott told him. He peered through the telescope, adjusting several

107

knobs. "I hear you're interested in science, Bobby. Lucky tells me you know just about everything about spiders."

"I wish," Bobby said. "The more I read, the more I find out how much I don't know."

"That's true about space, too," Mr. Prescott said. "Maybe it's true about everything."

"This is the best night we've had in a while," Lucky said to Bobby. "Last week we had a clear night like this, but there was a big old moon messing everything up."

"What's wrong with the moon?" Bobby asked.

"Nothing," Mr. Prescott said. "But if you want to look farther, at the planets and stars, you won't have much luck because the moonlight is so bright it washes everything else away. There. Have a look, Bobby."

Bobby looked through the eyepiece. Saturn! Saturn like he'd never seen it with rings of green and blue, brilliant bands in distinct shades of emerald green and aqua and sapphire blue. And a black ring in the middle. It stunned him that something so far away could be so clear and sharp.

"There's supposed to be about a thousand different rings around Saturn," Lucky said as he stepped away from the telescope. Sam jumped up to the eyepiece.

"I'm gonna go to Saturn," Sam exclaimed. "Definitely."

"You wouldn't have any place to stand," Lucky said. "It's nothing but gas."

"Wouldn't need to stand," Sam replied. "I'd fly around with my portable power pack. Hey, Dad, can you find us a DSO?"

"DSO?" Bobby asked.

"A deep space object," Lucky explained. "Can you find one, Dad?"

"Hang on," Mr. Prescott said after a moment. "Here, Bobby. Feast your eyes on that."

This time Bobby saw a swatch of tiny dots or bubbles, countless bright spots in a swirl of pinks, magentas, indigos.

"That's Andromeda, the closest galaxy to our Milky Way," Mr. Prescott told him. "You're looking at a galaxy with billions of stars, two million light years away."

They took turns looking through the telescope until Sam got bored and went inside. Then the phone rang, and Mr. Prescott left to take the call. For a minute Bobby and Lucky just sat there looking up at the stars.

"So what do spiders do at night?" Lucky finally asked. Bobby shrugged.

"Lots of things. For a spider, nighttime is where the action is. Some repair their webs. Lots go hunting. There are more bugs out at night than during the day."

"Do spiders dream?"

"You ask the strangest questions, you know

that?" Lucky had moved next to him, her arm touching his. But when the bedroom door slid open, she quickly moved away from him.

"All right!" Mr. Prescott said, rubbing his hands together. "What should we look for next, Lucky?"

"Whatever," she said. In the darkness Bobby could see that she was smiling at him.

Ten

October 11

Dance, Dance, Dance. Seems like all anybody talks about in school these days is the Seventh Grade Halloween Dance. I walked past Chick Hall in the library yesterday and heard him yapping to some girl about it. What's the big deal?

All this talk about the big dance reminds me of something I read in one of my spider books.

In the 1600s, in Italy, doctors believed that people who got bit by a tarantula could catch a disease they called "tarentism." The symptoms of tarentism were pain and swelling, paralysis, vomiting, delirium, palpitations, fainting, "shameless exhibitionism," and depression. People who had tarentism often died.

Supposedly the only way to cure tarentism was for the sick person to dance wildly for hours and hours until that person was covered with sweat.

For a long time scientists argued about tarentism. Was it a real disease or just a hoax? There haven't been any cases reported for many years. But today in Italy women still do a dance called the tarantella.

On Monday night, Bobby went back to Lucky's house. Mr. Prescott had just locked the telescope onto Neptune when the phone in his bedroom began to ring.

"I've been waiting for this call," he said, stepping away from the telescope. "Help yourself. I'm going to be a little while."

After he went inside, Bobby and Lucky took turns looking at Neptune. Then they sat next to each other on the bench.

"Want to play a game?" Lucky asked softly.

"Like what?"

"I don't know. How about Truth or Dare?"

"Huh?" He looked at her.

"Don't tell me you've never played Truth or Dare," she said. "Don't they have that game in Illinois? There's different ways of playing. The simplest way is that I get to ask you a question,

112

anything, and you've got to answer. Even if it's your biggest, baddest secret. Then you get to ask me something."

"I don't know," he said uncertainly.

"C'mon, it's fun," Lucky said.

"All right," he said. "But I go first."

"Okay, shoot."

"Raise your right hand," he ordered. "Do you solemnly swear to tell the truth-the-whole-truth-and-nothing-but-the-truth-so-help-you-God?"

"I do, I do." Lucky giggled.

"Hmmm." A question popped into his mind, but he didn't know exactly how to ask it.

"I'm waiting," she said.

"Okay, okay, here goes. What did you think about that thing I wrote about the silk farm?"

"That was good." Lucky nodded.

"That's not what I mean. I mean, like, what did you think when you found out I made the whole thing up? What did you *really* think?"

"Anansi," she said without hesitation.

"Huh?"

"Anansi the Spider Man," she explained. "It's an African folk tale. The sky god was hoarding all the stories of the world for himself. Anansi wanted to share those stories with all the people, but first the sky god made Anansi perform three tasks, hard ones. And when Anansi did them all, well, the sky god let him bring a box of stories down to the people. That's how we have stories today."

"Yeah, right." He half-remembered a picture book he'd read about Anansi.

"Can I call you Anansi?"

"Nope."

"Well, I'm still going to *think* of you as Anansi. The spider boy who brings stories. Now. My turn." She rubbed her hands in anticipation. "This is a two-part question."

"That's not fair!" he protested.

"Relax, don't have a hairy canary, you can, too, if you want." She cleared her throat. "Have you ever been friends before with someone who's black?"

"What?" he asked. The question caught him off guard. "Well, yeah, sure, sort of. In Illinois. Why?"

"I don't know," Lucky said. For a few seconds she didn't say anything. "It's strange. I'm black, and I know how that feels. But I don't know what it feels like to be not-black. Even though I try to imagine it. Maybe I think about it too much, but well, it's like . . . I don't know. I mean, do you think of me as Lucky-the-girl-who-is-black? Or do you think about me as plain Lucky?"

"Am I allowed to think," Bobby asked, "or do I have to answer right away?"

"Right away or you forfeit your turn." She elbowed him.

"Ouch! Plain Lucky, then."

"Have you ever kissed a girl?" she asked him.

"Hey, it's my turn."

114

"Have you?"

"Nope," he said. "Well, not really."

"Not really? C'mon. 'Fess up."

"There was one time, last year, but it doesn't really count," he said.

"Tell me. I want to hear every juicy detail."

"It was dumb. I was staying over at my friend Mike's house. He has a sister, Melanie, a couple years older than me. Me and Mike stayed up talking about stuff until, like, two in the morning. Then I said something and he didn't answer. He'd fallen asleep. His sister Melanie answered instead. Her bedroom is right next to Mike's. She said, 'C'mere, you can see Orion's Belt perfectly through my window.' So I went over, and while we were standing there she tried to kiss me. I just went back to Mike's room and fell asleep."

"That doesn't count," Lucky said softly. To his great astonishment she kissed him on the mouth, right there on the deck outside her parents' bedroom. Bobby didn't know what to say.

*

Mr. Prescott drove him home. Bobby perched nervously in the front seat. He wondered if a father had a sixth sense that told him if a boy had been kissing his daughter. The man stayed quiet during the entire drive. Maybe he's mad at me, Bobby thought.

"So what do you think of the telescope?" Mr.

115

Prescott asked when he pulled up to Bobby's house.

"It's great," Bobby said. "It opens up a whole new world."

"For me, looking at the stars puts things into perspective," Mr. Prescott said. He leaned back and scratched his beard. "When you look up at Andromeda galaxy, you realize that we're just the tiniest speck in this universe."

"Yes, sir." Bobby tried the door handle, but the door was locked.

"I hope you'll come again," Mr. Prescott said, unlocking the door.

"Me, too. Thanks a lot."

He got out of the car and hurried into the house.

October 11 (second entry)

If spiders are such solitary creatures, how do the males and females ever find each other? I've been reading stuff on how tarantulas mate. Captive spiders in a small tank can't avoid each other but in open wild spaces it must be much harder to find a mate.

Most male spiders wander more than females, so it's usually the males who find the females. They find a silk thread and they can tell right away if it was made by a female spider from their own species, and whether the female is ready to mate. If so, they follow that thread.

But finding a mate can be dangerous—especially for the male who is usually smaller and weaker than the female. Spiders are always ready to kill and eat almost any insect or small animal that comes within range. And they won't hesitate to eat each other.

When male spiders want to get together with female spiders they act in special ways to avoid being mistaken for just another juicy bug.

Some male spiders pluck the web of a female spider in a certain rhythm to let her know he's a friendly male who wants to mate.

The male of one species (Xysticus) protects himself during mating by fastening the female to the ground with silk threads.

When a male nursery web spider thinks he has found Miss Right he captures a fly, wraps it up, and gives it to her. She unwraps and eats his present—this gives him just enough time to mate with her. And escape.

A male crab spider ties up a female spider and

while she's still wrapped up he is able to mate with her safely. After he leaves, she unties herself.

Consider how the black widow got its name. The female allows the male to mate with her. And to show her appreciation she kills him. Eats him. This isn't some kind of fairy tale: it's a scientific fact.

It's lucky that human girls aren't this dangerous. Or who knows—maybe they are.

Eleven

On Tuesday morning Bobby brought Monk to school. He used an aquarium net to carefully catch the big spider and transfer him to a small terrarium. It was a cold morning. Bobby asked Dad to start the car and crank up the heat so Monk wouldn't get chilled. He carried the terrarium into Mr. Niezgocki's lab and put it next to Thelma's. The door opened.

"Thought I might find you in here," Lucky said.

"Meet Monk," Bobby said. "He's the king baboon spider I was telling you about. Mr. N was curious about him so I brought him in."

"Man," she said, peering in. "You know, I think he's even uglier than Thelma."

"I think he's beautiful," Bobby said.

"I know, but you're crazy," she reminded him.

"I can't keep him filled up. He loves those crickets."

"Oh please," she moaned, "I just had breakfast. Hey, what would happen if you put him in with Thelma? Would they, like, make lots of ugly babies?"

"He's pretty aggressive. You should hear the hissing sound he makes sometimes. No, I don't think Thelma would last long in a tank with him. Anyway, it wouldn't work. They're not the same species."

"They're not?" She bent closer. "Looks like a tarantula to me."

"Yeah, he is, but he's from Africa and she's from South America. Can't you see the difference? They—"

"You and me don't look alike either," Lucky said, putting her arm along his arm, dark skin and light. "Aren't we the same species?"

"Course we are," he said.

"All right, then."

"But it's different with tarantulas."

"Okay, it's different." She shrugged. "Hey, wish me luck today. This is my big day."

"Huh?"

"The big race after school. If it doesn't rain. Wish me luck."

"Good luck. Think you've got a chance?"

"A very slim one," she said with a sly grin.

"You're so darned sure of yourself," he said. "What if somebody beats you? It could happen, you know."

120

"I know," she said, deadpan.

"And?"

"I figure I can always become a cheerleader. Or a pom-pom girl."

"Yeah, right."

"Hey, listen." She looked down. "About last night. You know, what happened . . . I was thinking we should stay . . . friends. You know?"

"Yeah," he said, nodding.

"I'm still getting used to this crazy place," Lucky said. "I'm not ready for a boyfriend right now. Are you?"

"Ready for a boyfriend?" Bobby laughed. "No, I don't think so."

"You know what I mean!" She offered her hand. "Friends?"

"Friends," he said.

They shook hands very formally and burst out laughing.

When Lucky left the lab, Bobby took a deep breath. She was right. He felt a huge wave of relief. But he also felt the tiniest sliver of something else. Sadness, maybe. Or regret.

*

"Clear your desks for the test," Mr. Niezgocki said at the beginning of science class. Groans. Mr. Niezgocki stood at the front of the room holding a thick pile of test papers.

"As you all know we've just begun a new honor

system, and that's going to mean a few changes in the way we do things around here. I will no longer act as a policeman during a test. You're too old for that, and so am I. I trust you to behave yourselves. I may leave the room for a few minutes while you're taking the test. Under the honor system you'll have more freedom, but there is also more responsibility put on you to be honest and to insure that your peers are being honest."

Somebody snickered from the back of the room. Mr. Niezgocki glared at him.

"Do you find that funny, Mr. Carroll?"

"No," the boy said.

"This is an experiment. I think it's important. It's not very often you get to shape the kind of school you go to. It's up to you. If it doesn't work, if people abuse it, we'll go back to the old way of teachers babysitting students. I hope that doesn't happen."

The geology test packet came to Bobby. Question number one: *Describe at least three different terrains a river might pass through from its source water to the ocean. Describe the interplay between the river and this terrain. Specifically, how does the river affect the terrain? In what ways does the terrain affect the river?* Question number two: *Name three ways glaciers permanently changed the landscapes through which they passed.*

122

Bobby gulped.

He started to write, dredging up from memory the answers he knew or thought he knew. After about ten minutes he realized that Mr. Niezgocki had left the room. Other kids looked up, realized they were alone, and went back to work. It felt weird to be sitting in a roomful of kids his age with no adult around. And nobody talking.

Then Bobby spotted Chick Hall at the front of the room, leaning to his left and furiously copying off Scott Shanahan's test paper. Scott's paper was pushed all the way to the right so Chick could get a good look at the answers.

Bobby felt a flush of anger. Scott was one of those popular, tough kids who still managed to get high grades. Chick Hall would ace this test simply by copying Scott's answers.

Cheating. And no teacher around to see it, let alone stop it.

Bobby glanced over at Lucky. She met his gaze and rolled her eyes at him, but he realized she only meant how hard the test was. From her seat, she probably couldn't see Chick at all.

When Mr. Niezgocki returned to the room, Chick's gaze snapped back to his own test. Mr. Niezgocki stayed for five minutes, but when he left again Chick's eyes flew back to Scott's test. He started copying some more, his pencil moving even faster than before. Nobody else seemed to notice it.

Bobby glanced up and saw that he'd already wasted at least ten minutes. *Forget about Chick*, he told himself. *You can't do a thing about that. Concentrate! Think rock! Faults and folds. Plate tectonics. Sedimentary rocks are made in layers. Fossils are often found in sedimentary rocks. Igneous and metamorphic rocks—one made from fire, the other through pressure. Which is which?* He worked hard to catch up, moving swiftly, trying not to make careless errors.

"Time's up," Mr. Niezgocki announced. Kids looked up, blinked, groaned. Bobby still had two questions to go.

"That was *hard*, Mr. N," one boy said.

Chick Hall stretched and loudly cracked his knuckles.

"Before you pass in your test, there's something you need to read on the bottom of the last page," Mr. Niezgocki said. "It says, 'On my honor I know of no cheating on this test.' Under the new honor system, whenever you take a test you must read that and sign your name below it. If you are aware of cheating on this test, you should sign your name and *draw a line through your signature*. Is that clear? Sign your name no matter what. You may hand me your test on the way out of the room."

On my honor I know of no cheating on this test. On my honor I know of no cheating on this test. On my honor. Bobby read and reread those

124

words. Each time they brought back the picture of Chick copying off Scott's paper.

He signed his name. And drew a dark line through it.

"That was a bear!" Lucky whispered outside the room.

"It was easier for some people than for others," Bobby said.

"Meaning you?" she asked.

"Forget it."

"I'm depressed," Lucky told him.

"The test?"

"Look," Lucky said. She pointed to a window through which they could see rain spattering the dark asphalt outside the cafetorium. "No race. Like I said, when I can't run, I get glum."

*

After school Bobby found Mr. Niezgocki waiting for him in the lab, a serious expression on his face.

"Sit down," he said. "I just saw your test paper."

"How'd I do?" Bobby asked.

"You know what I'm talking about."

"Yeah." Bobby lowered his eyes.

"You know, Bobby, I was one of the people here who really pushed for this honor system," Mr. Niezgocki said. He stood and began pacing back and forth. "Lots of teachers thought kids in this school weren't ready for it. I argued that it was just what kids needed. I still think so. I really want it to work here. It's so important to give you young people choices here, now, where we can help you see the consequences of those choices."

Bobby looked at him.

"You're *sure* you saw somebody cheating?" Mr. Niezgocki asked. "Could you possibly have been mistaken?"

"Mistaken?"

"A few weeks ago you wrote an imaginative essay about your father's silk farm." Mr. Niezgocki folded his arms. "That turned out to be fiction. Just wondering if this might be another fiction."

"You think this is just another story I'm making up." Bobby looked down at the floor.

"Is it?" the man asked.

"No!" Bobby replied sharply. "You don't have to believe me. But I'm telling the truth."

"I do believe you," Mr. Niezgocki said glumly. "I wish I didn't, but I do."

"Did anybody else cross out their names?"

"No." Mr. Niezgocki sighed. "I have to admit I'm curious about who it is you saw cheating. But I should tell you that you don't have to name the person. You've already done everything you're supposed to do."

"I'd rather not say," Bobby said after a moment.

"I see."

"I guess maybe I shouldn't have crossed out my name," Bobby said.

"No," Mr. Niezgocki said. "You did the right thing, young man. But sometimes doing the right thing puts other people in a tough spot."

*

Next morning on the way to science class, Bobby heard a familiar cry.

"Hey, Spider Boy!" It was Chick Hall with a gang of three. "How's the spider business? Eat any good bugs lately?"

Raucous laughter. Bobby tried to move around him, but Chick blocked his way.

"C'mon, Spider Boy, don't be like that," Chick said. "You know, I'm your biggest fan! I got all your comics!"

All at once Chick lurched forward and pushed Bobby in the chest. Bobby could see himself as if in slow motion, falling backward over someone who had knelt behind him, his books and notebooks spilling all over the place.

"Nice trip?" Chick asked, extending his hand. Bobby ignored it. He gathered his books and got up, flustered but unhurt.

"Hey, Chick," he said, motioning him closer. When Chick drew close enough Bobby whispered, "I got a new nickname for you. Chick the Cheat."

Chick stepped back like he'd been struck.

"What'd he say?" Scott Shanahan asked Chick

as Bobby turned and walked into Mr. Niezgocki's class.

*

Mr. Niezgocki had a murderous expression on his face as students filed into his classroom. He sat on the corner of his desk with two stacks of papers beside him.

"Bad news, guys." He pointed at one stack of papers. "Yesterday someone in this class saw cheating. On this test."

Gasps.

"Cheating." Mr. Niezgocki stood up and paced, letting the sound of the word spread through the classroom. "Cheating. And I have no good reason not to believe the person who reported it. I take this very seriously. Cheating gives one person an unfair advantage over the honest students in this class. It is wrong and I will not tolerate it."

He looked out at the class. Nobody moved.

"Here's what is going to happen. I'm going to give you the test again. We are going to have to spend valuable class time doing something we've already done." He pointed at the second stack of papers. "We will begin now. Same material, just different questions. This time I will stay in the room to monitor you."

There was a chorus of groans as he began passing out the tests.

"It's not fair!" someone muttered. "I didn't cheat!"

"Absolutely no talking!" Mr. Niezgocki said.

Bobby sat, frozen. He took a deep breath. Lucky looked over at him, rolling her eyes as if to say, "Can you believe this?" Several kids swiveled around angrily, raking the class with accusing eyes that asked, "Who squealed?"

He couldn't see Chick's face. Bobby kept hoping that Chick would glance back at him, just once, but Chick kept his face and body hunched forward the whole time. When the bell rang, Chick handed in his test and bolted from the room.

*

That afternoon Bobby and Butch hurried outside to watch the race. The rain had stopped; there was a slight chill in the air. Bobby watched Lucky stretching at the side of the track. She was wearing her headband and dark blue racing trunks. It wasn't hard at all to imagine her in the Olympics. He could clearly picture it, Lucky Prescott being interviewed by a famous sports broadcaster:

"Congratulations on your fine run, Lucky. I understand that there's a story behind your name. Is that right?"

"Well, yes, as a matter of fact . . ."

129

The track was crowded; practically the whole school had turned out to watch the race.

"When I play chess, I like to go for the quick kill," Butch said. "Does Lucky have a strategy when she runs?"

"I guess we'll find out," Bobby replied.

Lucky broke into the lead at the start of the race. By the half-mile mark she had opened a big lead.

"Go! Go!" Bobby and Butch screamed as she streaked past.

A giddy feeling began to spread inside Bobby as he watched. Boy, could she run! No one, not even the eighth-grade boys, could keep up with her. She streaked around the track, her face calm and relaxed as if to say, *Hey, no big deal. This is easy. Fun.* She finished another lap, and another, striding effortlessly, pulling farther and farther ahead of the rest of the pack.

"Ballenger!" It was Scott Shanahan. "Chick's looking for you!"

"So what?" Bobby asked, keeping his eyes on the track. Right then Chick Hall showed up and roughly wedged himself between Bobby and Butch.

"Well if it isn't Spider Boy and his famous sidekick, the Worm. You here to be cheerleader for your girlfriend, Spider Boy?"

"She's not my girlfriend. Chick." Bobby glared at him, letting the other two words—*the Cheat*—

hang unspoken in the air. "And you really should come up with some new material. Those Spider Boy jokes are getting awful tired, don't you think?"

"I know what you did," Chick hissed, putting his finger in Bobby's face. "Just want you to know that you're dead."

"Oh, really?"

"Really." Chick stepped so close Bobby could smell his breath. "Mark this down in your diary. You're a dead man."

"We all have to go sometime, right?" Bobby asked, shrugging. He turned to Butch. "What do you say we go congratulate Lucky?"

"But the race isn't over," Butch said.

"Believe me, it's over." Bobby turned and started walking toward the finish line.

"A dead man!" Chick yelled after them.

October 13

The world is dangerous for spiders, too. People think of them as ferocious predators who don't have a care in the world. Truth is spiders are surrounded by predators who will kill and eat them lickety split.

Spiders get eaten by small birds. They get fed to baby birds still in the nest. Lots of birds like to use spider egg cocoons to line their nests.

A major enemy of spiders: other spiders! When baby spiders hatch and the food runs out they get eaten by their own brothers and sisters.

There's one kind of spider (Mimetus) that lives by eating only other spiders.

Man is the biggest threat to spiders. People. We cut down rainforests where they live. We capture them and sell them as pets. And we use lots of insecticides in farming—that poisons spiders, too. Whatever poisons an insect ends up poisoning the spider who eats that insect.

In parts of the world PEOPLE ACTUALLY EAT SPIDERS!!!

Native people in Laos eat two different types of large spiders. They get roasted, dipped into salt, their legs pulled off. Supposedly the abdomen tastes like raw potato and lettuce mixed. Yum yum.

When a predator attacks a spider the first thing it does is to try to remove the spider from its home environment. Web spiders can't protect themselves nearly so well when they are torn away from their webs.

Like me. Here I am in New Paltz, pulled far from

my real friends, my real home. Chick Hall is threatening me. Funny, but I don't feel any danger. I'm not afraid of him. Maybe I should be— but I'm not.

Twelve

Bobby woke with Chick's words—*you're dead*—stuck like wax in his ears.

Chick wanted him to be afraid, to feel fear. But he didn't feel afraid. He had read that animals could smell fear. He wondered if that were true. Could a tarantula smell fear on a small lizard? Could a lion detect the odor of fear on a sickly wildebeest? What did fear smell like? Maybe fear had a foul smell, like a partially decayed animal. Maybe to a predator fear smelled delicious, like roast pork with garlic mashed potatoes. Or a feta cheese omelette.

His stomach growled. He bounded out of bed and down the stairs without even bothering to get out of his pajamas.

"I'm hungry," he announced in the kitchen.

"Well, it's about time!" Mom said with a grin.

She was watching the morning news on the small TV sitting on the breakfast bar. The newscaster looked grim as he reported an earthquake somewhere in the Pacific. Fault, Bobby thought, imagining those immense rock plates sliding apart beneath billions of tons of water. "How about I make you an omelette?"

"An omelette?" He couldn't believe his ears. He couldn't remember the last time Mom had made breakfast for him. Or for anyone else in the family, for that matter.

"Sure, why not?" Mom said, shrugging. "I'm in a good mood—three miles again today, no problem. How hard could it be to make one little cheese omelette?"

"Great. Hey, where is everybody?"

"Dad had an early meeting. Luke took Breezy to the diner for breakfast."

He watched Mom put a slab of butter into the omelette pan. While the butter melted, she cracked three eggs into a coffee mug and began to whisk the eggs together. His nose twitched at the smell of the melting butter.

"I need to stop at the post office on the way to school," she said.

"That's okay," Bobby said. "I don't need a ride."

She looked at him, surprised.

"Why not?"

"I dunno." He shrugged. "It's barely a mile. From now on I'm going to walk."

He didn't see Chick Hall all morning, not in homeroom or science class. After lunch he went outside. Pure Indian Summer—one of those sunny fall days when every leaf and shadow seemed to be in perfect focus. Kids were wearing T-shirts and shorts, sitting in groups or strolling around. He wandered toward a soccer game on the far side of the rec field.

"Spider Boy!"

Suddenly Chick Hall stood in front of him with four or five other kids standing behind.

"This is for you," Chick said and without warning he lunged at Bobby and caught him in the chest. Chick tackled him down, rolled him over. Shouts erupted around them.

"Get him, Chick!" somebody yelled. "Punch his lights out!"

Bobby grabbed Chick by the collar and swung his weight, trying to continue the momentum and roll Chick over. But Chick was strong. He quickly put him into a tight headlock, crushing the tips of his ears against his head. Bobby struggled but couldn't move.

"You spider freak!" Chick hissed. "You told him, didn't you? Didn't you?"

Bobby couldn't speak; he could barely breathe.

All at once he felt Chick flipping over, the arms pulled from their stranglehold on his neck. Bobby

136

gulped in a breath and looked up. Lucky. She stood there, arms folded, scowling down at Chick.

"What do you guys think you're doing?" Lucky asked. Bobby staggered to his feet.

"What are *you* doing here?" he asked. His voice sounded hoarse, his throat hurt.

She looked at Bobby, then at Chick.

"C'mere," she said in a low voice. "I want to talk to you." She grabbed Bobby's arm and pulled, but Bobby didn't move.

"No!" he told her.

"You better—"

"Don't you get it?" he told her. "I don't want you here!"

Lucky stared at him. And all at once she was gone, sprinting toward the school.

"She's gonna tell a teacher!"

Bobby turned to Chick just in time to see a fist screaming toward his left eye. In that clear autumn light Bobby could see the punch arriving in perfect detail, the fist against Chick's white T-shirt, a line of white knuckles streaking toward his face—then BAM! Bobby went down, not with stars in his head the way it happened on cartoons but with bright streaks of dancing light. His head bounced heavily on the ground. The smell of grass filled his nose. Dazed and nauseous, he got to his knees. Lunch rose in his belly.

Whatever you do, he told himself, *don't throw up*. He rolled over. Chick's face leered down.

"Let's get out of here!" somebody yelled.

"It's not over yet," Chick said, "because you're still not dead."

*

The nurse gave him an ice pack to put on the lump above his eye.

"How'd you get that?" she asked.

"Head-on collision in the soccer game," Bobby told her.

"Oh, I see," she retorted. "And did you happen to notice what kind of truck you collided with?"

She muttered something to herself, jotted notes on a chart, and led him to a cot where he could lie down. Bobby found that when he closed his eyes he could watch the whole thing all over again on instant replay: the four knuckles flying toward his head, those bright streaks of dancing light.

He'd never had a real fight before. Only once in Naperville he had been close to getting into one, when Teddy Pelligrino threatened to clock him for something during an intramural basketball game. Bobby had walked away; Teddy apologized later in the day.

Bobby glanced at his watch: exactly twelve o'clock in Naperville. That meant the noon whistle was blowing, loud and shrill. At exactly this moment Mike and Chad were on the playground

138

holding their hands tight over their ears. Bobby's head throbbed.

"You're going to have that egg for a day or so," the nurse told him. "You want to go home? You want to call your parents?"

"No, I'm okay."

At the end of the day Lucky saw him at his locker.

"Hey, thanks for not telling," he told her.

"Thanks for nothing," she told him, biting her lower lip. "You guys can be such jerks, you know that?"

"What's with you?"

"I hate fighting! It's so stupid!"

"Hey wait a sec, you think *I* started it?"

She frowned at him.

"Listen, tonight I'm going to call you, and I want to hear the whole story. The *real* story."

He watched Lucky run off to track practice. Somebody grabbed him by the arm. Butch Fostick.

"Hey! I heard Chick Hall jumped you. You okay?"

"It was no big deal," Bobby said, walking into Mr. Niezgocki's laboratory.

"That's not what I heard," Butch said, slipping in with him.

"Well, you heard wrong," Bobby said. "You know how people exaggerate."

He bent down to check Thelma. It soothed him

139

to look at the tarantula and know that her world was totally different from his own. Totally separate. He put on the rubber gloves and reached into Monk's cage.

"You know, I've got a theory about fighting," Butch said. "The way I see it, the guys who—"

The door opened. Chick Hall walked in with Scott Shanahan and two other kids.

"Thought we'd find you here, Spider Boy!" The door shut. Chick smiled and took a step closer.

"Mr. N'll be here in about half a minute," Butch told Chick. "You better get out of here!"

"Mr. N's at a faculty meeting upstairs in the library," Chick said, smiling at Bobby. "C'mon, spider freak, let's you and me finish what we started."

Bobby proceeded to pick up Monk. *Dangerous and aggressive, can deliver a nasty bite.* He was grateful he had on the gloves. Monk seemed to freeze.

"Try it," Bobby said, holding Monk up to Chick. Chick jumped back a step. "But I wouldn't want to get my friend here mad if I were you."

"Yeah, sure," Chick said. "In class you told everyone they weren't dangerous. Remember, stupid?"

"Ever heard of an African king baboon spider?" Bobby asked. "I didn't think so. You know what the word *lethal* means? How about *fatal*? Look those words up in your Webster's. This is one of the deadliest spiders on earth."

140

Bobby took another step closer; Chick jumped back again.

"In Africa they call it a two-step spider. Know what that means? Well, I'm going to tell you what it means. If this spider bites you, you've got two steps before you're dead."

Pause.

"Yeah, right," Chick said. "How come you're holding it then?"

"Why do you think I'm wearing gloves, Einstein?" Bobby asked.

Right on cue, Monk raised his feelers and front feet and started making a dangerous hissing sound.

"Yeah, go ahead, Chick," Butch said. He was grinning. "Who knows? Maybe he's only bluffing."

"I think it's time for you guys to leave," Bobby said. "Show's over. You're starting to make him nervous."

He took a step closer to them. The other boys moved toward the door.

"Let's go," someone said.

"Just don't think it's over, Spider Boy," Chick said on the way out. "'Cause it's not."

*

That night Lucky called right after supper. Bobby told her the whole story—watching Chick cheat on the test, crossing out his signature, talk-

141

ing with Mr. Niezgocki, fighting with Chick, confronting Chick after school in the laboratory.

"Wow," she said after a long pause. "A two-step spider, huh? You make that up?"

"Yeah."

"That's pretty good." She laughed softly. "Thank God you can make up stuff like that on the spot. Weren't you afraid Monk might turn around and bite you?"

"A little. I was wearing protective gloves."

"I guess you're lucky, too."

"I guess," he said, though he didn't feel very lucky. He took a breath. "Would you have done what I did?"

"What? Snitch on Chick?"

"I didn't snitch!" he snapped. He hated hearing that word—*snitch*—come from her mouth. "Geez, Lucky. I didn't even tell Mr. Niezgocki it was Chick."

"I know, I know. But maybe you should've told Chick that."

"Oh, that's right, how stupid of me," Bobby said. "I totally forgot that Chick's one of your best friends."

"That's not fair."

"Then why are you always apologizing for him?"

"I'm sorry," Lucky said. She didn't sound sorry.

"I better go," he said. "Bye."

"Bye."

*

The next day he didn't see much of Lucky. Chick ignored him all day. But at 3 P.M., in homeroom, Chick looked over and Bobby saw a tiny smile on his face. By the time the bell rang, Bobby had an odd feeling in his stomach. He was the first one out of homeroom. He raced down the corridor and slipped into Mr. Niezgocki's laboratory. Thelma was resting as usual in the back of her terrarium. But Monk's terrarium was empty.

"Monk!" He bent down to take a closer look into Monk's terrarium. Then he checked Thelma's. No sign of Monk.

Lucky walked in.

"Monk's gone!" he shouted. He started ripping open drawers, closets, boxes.

"Check those plants!" he told Lucky. Bobby opened the heavy door to the refrigerator. Then he yanked open the freezer.

He saw it. The green fish net. Dark shape entangled inside.

"Oh no." He pulled out the net and saw Monk, lifeless, partially covered with sand.

"My God!" Lucky whispered. She covered her mouth.

Bobby put the cold spider onto a table. *What to do?* Not one of his spider books had ever mentioned how to bring a frozen tarantula back to

life. Or if you could. *Help!* Think-spiderthinkspi-
derthinkspiderthinkspiderthinkspider.   Think!
Bobby started blowing gently onto the spider's
body. The door opened.

"Somebody put Monk in the freezer!" Lucky
cried to Mr. Niezgocki.

"What?!"

Bobby concentrated on blowing, trying to keep
his breath warm, gentle, steady. Someone must
have come into the lab right after the last period
just before homeroom. Homeroom lasted ten
minutes. Ten minutes. He could see that the body
wasn't frozen solid. There was a chance, maybe
one in a thousand.

"Any idea who—" Mr. Niezgocki began.

"Look!" Bobby said. One of Monk's hairy legs
jumped.

"He moved!" Lucky cried.

"Help me," Bobby whispered. Lucky and Mr.
Niezgocki hurried over. The three leaned their
heads together, blowing softly on Monk. Another
of Monk's legs twitched, and another.

"He's alive!" Lucky cried again. "He's going to
make it!"

But suddenly all of Monk's legs folded together
in a spasm that left the spider motionless, and
Bobby knew for certain that he was dead.

Thirteen

Mr. Hall strode like a cowboy into the guidance office. He was a tall gray-haired man with wide shoulders and an ash-colored suit that looked expensive. He glanced at the people sitting around the table—Miss Davenport, Mr. Niezgocki, Dad, Bobby, and Chick. Miss Davenport introduced Mr. Hall to the other people in the room. He shook hands, nodding grimly.

"I want to talk to my son," Mr. Hall said, giving Chick a straight look. "Alone."

"You may use my office," Miss Davenport said.

Bobby watched Chick follow his father out of the room. *You may use my office.* He could see that it would be that kind of formal meeting.

They waited for Chick and Mr. Hall to return. Miss Davenport mentioned to Dad the unusually warm weather, his father smiled politely and said something back, but the rest of the time they all waited without speaking. Mr. Niezgocki corrected a stack of test papers. Bobby kept his eyes focused on a blank note pad at the center of the table so he wouldn't have to look at any of the adults in the room. Once Bobby heard what sounded like Mr. Hall's deep voice raised in anger from the next room.

The door opened. Mr. Hall came in first, with Chick close behind. It looked like he'd been crying.

"Sit right there," Mr. Hall ordered, pointing at an empty chair. Chick sat down. Mr. Hall looked even more furious than before. He took the chair next to Miss Davenport. She cleared her throat.

"I have something to say," Mr. Hall announced.

"It might be best," Miss Davenport said quietly, "if I first lay out the facts of this matter, as best as we can figure them."

"All right," Mr. Hall said, nodding.

"We're here because Bobby's pet tarantula was killed. I think there's some background to this incident that's important to look at so we can establish a context for what happened today." She opened her notebook and glanced down. "At the beginning of the year, Bobby was a new boy in school. He moved here from Illinois. Apparently during the past month Chick has been hostile to Bobby. He and some friends gave Bobby a nickname—Spider Boy—because of Bobby's interest in spiders. But they kept using it even when

146

Bobby asked them not to. There has been a pattern of taunting and teasing."

"Is this true?" Mr. Hall asked Chick.

Chick shrugged helplessly.

"If I might continue," Miss Davenport said. "As you may know, we've just introduced a new honor system here at the middle school. Among other things, this new system may put students in unmonitored testing situations. And it asks students to report cheating on tests. This week, on Tuesday, Bobby reported witnessing cheating on a geology test in Mr. Niezgocki's class. The class had to retake the test on Wednesday, and some students were quite angry. Isn't that right, Paul?"

Mr. Niezgocki nodded.

"This seems to be the point where things started spinning out of control," Miss Davenport said. "Yesterday, on Thursday, Chick and Bobby were involved in a fight on the recreation field. Bobby went to the nurse and reported a head-on collision during a soccer match. But the nurse doubts this, and talked to several students who say they definitely saw Chick punch Bobby in the face. After school there was also some kind of confrontation in Mr. Niezgocki's lab, where Bobby sometimes works." She sighed and dropped her pencil. "Then there was what happened today."

Pause. Mr. Hall looked at Mr. Niezgocki. "Sir, are you telling me that my son cheated on your test?"

147

"I didn't say that," Mr. Niezgocki said. "And Bobby didn't either. He signed his name and crossed it out—that told me he had seen someone cheating. That afternoon I met with Bobby and asked him if he would tell me who it was. He refused to say. And he's not required to. The stipulations of the honor system are clear about that. But I have strong suspicions, especially after I saw the results of the re-test."

"What do you mean?"

"When someone's test score drops thirty points from one test to the other, on the same material, well, you know something's fishy."

Mr. Hall looked at Chick, who was studying something on the floor. For a long moment no one spoke. A giant waste of time, Bobby thought. All these words and ten million more won't give Monk one more second of life.

"Miss Davenport," Mr. Hall said, "has the school decided on a punishment?"

"No, not yet," Miss Davenport said. "Today Mr. Wagner is at a conference. He'll review the situation when he returns, and make a decision."

"I see," Mr. Hall said. "Well, I can tell you that whatever punishment the school hands out will be no more severe than what he'll get at my house. My wife and I are old-fashioned people who try hard to bring our kids up to be decent human beings. Words like *honesty, hard work,* and *integrity* mean something to me. Working hard to be the best you can be at whatever you do. It isn't easy bringing up kids these days, what with the junk they watch on TV and at the movies. But we try. I take this incident very seriously."

Nobody spoke.

"Bobby, I'm very sorry." Mr. Hall turned toward him. "I understand that this was a very special pet. I know it doesn't help much, but I will pay for this loss. And I can assure you my son will pay me back. Mr. Ballenger, please accept my apologies as well."

Stiffly, Dad nodded.

"How much does an . . . animal like this cost?" Mr. Hall asked. "I have no idea."

"I paid forty dollars for Monk," Dad said, looking at Bobby. "But I bought it from a friend at work—I understand that this kind of tarantula usually goes for about twice that much."

"Well, I suppose we're talking replacement value here," Mr. Hall said, reaching into his wallet. He pulled out four twenty-dollar bills. "Would you rather have a check?"

"No, cash is fine," Dad said with an uncomfortable shrug.

Bobby sat stone still. *Eighty dollars. Replacement value. Cash or check.* Talking about Monk like he was no more than a busted lawn mower.

"If Bobby has any more problems with my son, I want you to call me immediately," Mr. Hall said

149

to Dad. "Now, I believe my son has something to say."

"I'm really sorry," Chick said to Bobby. His voice sounded surprisingly clear, as if he'd been rehearsing this. "I guess it was an awful stupid thing to do."

Bobby didn't look at him.

"Well?" Dad said to Bobby after a moment. "Do you accept his apology?"

Bobby said nothing.

"Bobby?"

"No!" Bobby drew a deep breath, keeping his eyes focused on the middle of the table.

"Why not?" Dad asked.

"I just don't," Bobby said.

Pause.

"Why don't you guys shake hands and try to put this behind you," Dad said.

"No way!" Bobby said. He looked at Dad and his eyes said, *You can't make me.*

"Well, I suppose that's his right," Mr. Hall said. He stood up. "Is that all then?"

*

Dad started the engine and began backing out of the parking space. Neither one of them said anything all the way home. Dad pulled into the driveway and shut off the car. He sat there, hands still gripping the steering wheel.

"What did you think about Chick's father?"

150

"What do you mean?"

"I just wonder," Dad said. "Either that was one terrific acting job, or I wouldn't want to be Chick going home tonight."

Bobby stared straight ahead.

"I don't get it," Dad said at last. "This kid was bullying you, making your life miserable for over a month. Why didn't you say something to us about it?"

"It didn't seem like that much of a big deal."

Dad sighed and shook his head. "What *would* you consider a big deal?"

"What happened to Monk," he answered quietly. "*That's* a big deal."

Dad let out a breath.

"Look, what's done is done. Nothing can undo it. How come you wouldn't just accept an apology from this Chick Hall and be done with it?"

"I can't forgive him." Bobby shook his head.

"Acceptance isn't the same thing as forgiveness."

"No way," Bobby said.

*

He carried Thelma's terrarium into the house, past Mom and Breezy's questioning eyes and up to his bedroom. He brought Monk outside, took a spade from the shed, and dug a hole about a foot deep in a small clearing at the edge of the woods.

"I'm sorry," he whispered, kneeling down. Very

151

gently he placed Monk's body at the bottom of the hole and covered it with dirt.

During dinner Mom and Breezy listened to Dad try to explain what had happened. Bobby didn't speak.

"I'm so sorry, Bobby." Lightly, Mom touched his shoulder.

"Yeah," Breezy said. "That's, like, the worst."

"Mr. Hall was absolutely livid," Dad said. "I couldn't tell if he was really angry, or just sounding that way so they'd go easy on Chick."

"Mr. Hall has always been real nice to me," Breezy said. "But Luke says he's got a real Irish temper."

Dad handed him an envelope. Inside Bobby could see the green tips of the money. Blood money. He dropped it onto the table.

"I don't want it," Bobby said.

"All right," Dad said. He put the envelope back in his pocket.

After supper the telephone rang. Lucky.

"What happened?"

"Nothing." *Nothing but murder.*

"What happened, you know, at the office?"

"I can't," he said after a moment. "I just don't want to talk about it."

"Okay. Let me know when you do."

"Yeah," he said.

"I'm so sorry, Bobby."

"Yeah," he said again, and all at once he hated

having to play the role of the victim. All that use-
less pity.

*

Upstairs, Bobby found an envelope on his bed.
Inside there was a card and photograph. It was a
photograph of Bobby smiling and squatting
down next to the terrarium—a great shot of
Monk climbing up the inside glass. The card said,
*I'm really sorry about what happened. I know
you really cared about him. Breezy.*

He lay on the bed. Snapped off the light. Rolled
over onto his pillow and started to sob, pushing
his face deep into the pillow so no one would
hear.

*

In the middle of the night he woke up, wide
awake. He took out the spider journal, and started
to write:

October 15

*Why couldn't I just accept his apology and be
done with it?*

*1) Because it's too damn easy. Kiss and make up.
Shake hands and walk away.*

2) Because Chick killed Monk like he was some

oversized cockroach. He didn't mean a single word of what he said in Miss Davenport's office. He apologized for one reason only: because his father would have ripped off his arms if he didn't.

3) Because Monk came all the way from Africa, a tropical tarantula who met death in an airtight freezer. And that's a horrible way to die.

4) Because I had no right taking chances with Monk's life. I was responsible for protecting Monk, keeping him in a place where he'd be safe. How can I forgive Chick if I can't forgive myself?

6) Because it easily could have been Thelma. It was nothing but dumb luck Thelma didn't get killed instead.

Fourteen

October 22

Last night I saw a fisher spider on the side of the house. I'd seen pictures of them but I'd never seen one in real life. It was ugly and BIG! About three or four inches across but not skinny like a daddy longlegs. This sucker had a body an inch long and thick legs. Fisher spiders don't make webs. They're hunters, like wolf spiders or tarantulas. (I seriously doubt they'd make good pets.)

Seems like lots of big spiders come out in the fall. Wonder why. Could it be that they grow big from a whole summer feasting on insects? Or are there certain large species that come out every autumn? Check on this.

Life has been pretty boring: doing homework, working in the lab, taking care of Thelma, seeing Chick Hall with dry hair every morning. (He got booted off the swimming team.)

Dad tells me I should invite a friend over to the house. Mom tells me I should finish unpacking the stuff in my bedroom. Seems like I'm surrounded by grownups with nothing better to do than give me advice—Dad, Mom, Mr. Niezgocki, Miss Davenport.

Miss Davenport isn't too bad. I went to see her yesterday. She's not half as flaky as I first thought. She listens. She asked me to read her parts from my spider journal. She liked it. Said she never realized how intelligent spiders are.

That got me thinking. Spiders are intelligent, but it's so different from human intelligence. Spiders are born knowing how to make a web, how to balloon up into the air. It's in their genes, like how all birds know how to make a nest. They don't have to go to nest-building or web-making school. They just know.

With us it's all different. We can change the way we act. We can learn from what happens to us.

I keep thinking there must be something impor-

*tant I can learn from what happened to Monk.
But what?*

"No," Butch said. "No, no, no."

"Why not?" Bobby asked. They were playing chess during lunch; he had just moved out his bishop.

"See, bishops can move as far as they want diagonally," Butch explained. "This is the first thing they teach you in chess camp: *knights before bishops*. Knights are much slower—they need a head start. Move your knights out first."

"Chess camp?" Bobby smiled, pulled back his bishop, and slid his knight diagonally forward. "Whoa, that sounds like a wild and crazy place."

"Yeah, well, it's a lot wilder than you might think," Butch said, studying the board. He moved out his own knight. "Hey, how come you didn't come to the soc hop? It was the warm-up for the Halloween dance."

"Just didn't feel like it," Bobby said, pushing a pawn two spaces forward. "How was it?"

"It was okay," Butch said, shrugging. "Lucky was there."

"Yeah?" Bobby said. Butch matched his move: pawn to king four.

"Yeah. What happened, you guys break up?"

"We were never unbroken," Bobby said. "She's just a friend."

157

"I've got a theory about guys and girls who are forever saying they're just friends," Butch said.

"I don't doubt it." Now he moved out the king side bishop.

"Anyway, I saw her dancing with different people," Butch said. "I think once I saw her dancing with Chick Hall."

"Got any more good news?"

Butch shrugged. "Thought you said you didn't care."

"You're right, I don't. Your move."

*

That afternoon Bobby walked home in a drenching rain. He plodded along without boots or raincoat or hat, wondering how insects managed to find any shred of dryness on such a day. Cars cruised past. The weather had turned cold. He could feel the wetness seeping through his sweater and slacks, but he didn't quicken his pace. A car eased to a stop a few yards ahead of him. When he walked abreast of it, he saw the window on the passenger side slide open.

"Well, if it isn't Bobby Ballenger!"

Roland Prescott's smiling face beamed out at him.

"How about a lift?"

"Well, I don't mind walking." Bobby tried to hide the shiver in his teeth.

"Come on, you're getting soaked."

"All right," Bobby said. All at once he wanted nothing more than to get out of the rain and into the warmth of that car. The seats were soft and deep, leather maybe. As soon as Bobby got into the car he could see he was getting them wet. "Geez, sorry about that."

"Don't worry, it's only water," Mr. Prescott said. "You know, I've discovered a place that makes the finest hot chocolate this side of the Mason-Dixon. Would you like to join me for a cup?"

"Okay. Do you have a tissue I could borrow?"

"You can keep it," Mr. Prescott said, handing him one. Bobby blew his nose.

"Thank you."

"Lucky told me about what happened to your spider. I'm sorry about that, son." He shook his head.

"Yeah, thanks." *Thanks for what?*

"You know, some folks have about as much human kindness as a heartworm in an old dog."

"Have you been using your telescope?" Bobby asked. He was eager to change the subject.

"Oh, yes," Mr. Prescott said. "These clear nights have been great for stargazing, till today. I suppose we were due for a stretch of rain."

They pulled in front of what looked like a small café. A purple neon sign—CHINO'S—was lit above the door. Inside, the place smelled sweet and cinnamony. Mr. Prescott motioned to the corner booth.

159

"Like I said, they do serve some terrific hot chocolate, and chili, too, if you're hungry," Mr. Prescott said when they sat down. "Are you?"

Bobby shook his head, enjoying the warmth of the room. After a few moments, a stout woman appeared behind the counter.

"Hi, Maddy!" Mr. Prescott called. "Any chance you can rustle us up a couple of your famous hot chocolates? With a double helping of cream."

"Double creams," she repeated and disappeared. A minute later she brought over two enormous mugs crested with cream. Bobby took a sip. He had never, ever tasted anything so good.

"Ahh!" Mr. Prescott sipped and smacked his lips. "Almost as good as the cocoa my mom used to make. This was my favorite thing to drink after football practice—even better than Gatorade."

"You played football?" Bobby asked.

"Every chance I got. Junior high, high school. College, too, until I got injured."

"What position?"

"In high school I played quarterback. In college they moved me to halfback." Mr. Prescott took another sip. "How about you? Do you play?"

"Yes, I love football."

"Really?" Mr. Prescott smiled. "I guess I figured you for more of a one-on-one sport, like tennis. What position do you play?"

"Wide receiver," Bobby said. "I played on the sixth-grade team last year."

160

"Are you fast?"

"About average," Bobby said. "But I could get open. The coach said I was more quick than fast."

At this Roland Prescott banged the table and let out a laugh, a loud guffaw that startled Bobby.

"Don't you just love the way coaches talk? The things that come out of their mouths? Ha! What else did he say?"

"He said I had soft hands. That's good, right?"

"You bet it's good!" Mr. Prescott was excited now. "When I played QB I used to love to throw to receivers like you! Big guys who could get open and catch the ball! Are you playing any ball right now?"

"Just touch. They're starting a new tackle league and I want to play, but Mom doesn't like it. She says it's too dangerous."

"Can be," Mr. Prescott said. "Still, if you really want to play, you ought to sit down and talk to her."

"Yeah," Bobby said.

"Here's what I think," Mr. Prescott said, leaning back. He took off his glasses and used his napkin to rub clean the lenses. "Living in this crazy world of ours fills you up with so much junk—worries, tensions—you've got to find some way to empty yourself out. So you can start over, start fresh, and fill yourself up with all the good stuff life has to offer."

Bobby nodded. Another grown-up with advice to share. He was bone tired of advice.

"Some folks have fishing, or golf," Mr. Prescott was saying. "I used to have football—now I've got the stars. Lucky's got her running. What do you have?"

Bobby shrugged. What did he have? Thelma, his study of spiders, and a best friend who lived eleven hundred miles away. All at once it didn't seem like enough. He slipped his spoon into the cocoa but the mug was empty.

"Well, anyway, that's my lecture for the day. Hey, let's have one more, what do you say? Then we're going to get you home so you can get into some dry clothes."

"All right," Bobby said. The cocoa had warmed him from the inside out. Suddenly he felt a wave of drowsiness almost as delicious as that hot chocolate.

Fifteen

Thelma had split into two spiders. Bobby knelt
down and stared into the terrarium, but no matter how many times he blinked he kept seeing the
same thing. One Thelma was moving around in a
corner of the terrarium, and the other remained
hiding in the burrow tube he had bought for her
the previous week.

Half-panicked, half-excited, Bobby kept looking from one Thelma to the other. It didn't make
sense. He couldn't get a clear view of the Thelma
hiding in the tube, but the Thelma in the corner
of the tank looked terrific, almost brand-new. Her
hair glistened. She lifted her legs, restlessly trying
to climb the glass.

Bobby dropped a live cricket into the tank.
Thelma turned, raced over, and jumped on it. She
sank her fangs into the cricket and began to feast.

"Whoa," Bobby whispered.

He reached into the terrarium, carefully removed the burrow tube, and peered again at the Thelma inside. When he tipped the tube a brittle shell fell into his hand. Empty.

Suddenly it all made sense. Thelma had molted!

He raced downstairs.

"Look!" he cried in the kitchen. "Thelma's molted!"

"Congratulations," Breezy said from her perch at the breakfast bar. "Is that contagious?"

"Very funny."

"Is she all right?" Mom asked.

"Yeah, she's fine," Bobby said, showing them the spider shell. "It's kind of like how a snake sheds its skin when it gets too small, except this isn't skin, it's skeleton. See, spiders have their exoskeletons on the outside. When they get too big for their shells they just climb out and grow another. Baby spiders molt four or five times a year, big ones about once a year. You should see Thelma. She's beautiful!"

"I seriously doubt that," Breezy said.

"Yeah, well, she just ate a cricket. And it's practically the first thing she's eaten since we moved here."

"That's wonderful," Mom said. She hugged him. "Wonderful."

*

In school he hurried into Mr. Niezgocki's lab to show him Thelma's shell.

"Isn't that something?" Mr. Niezgocki said, turning the shell over and over.

"That's the exoskeleton, right?" Bobby asked.

"Yes, but I also want you to look up the word *carapace*," Mr. Niezgocki said. "Here. I'll write it down for you."

"You should see Thelma now. I mean, she looks so different. Younger. And she's got her appetite back."

"She's done what we all try to do," Mr. Niezgocki said, shaking his head. "Started over. Climbed out of her tired, old self and into a sleek new body. She's reinvented herself. Wouldn't it be great if it were that easy for us?"

Bobby nodded.

"Say, I've got to run for a meeting," Mr. Niezgocki said. "Do you have the time?"

Bobby glanced down at his watch. The digits flashed 7:43 A.M., Naperville time.

"It's really eight forty-three," Bobby said. "This watch is wrong."

*

After lunch he went outside. Another sunny day, colder than before. Bobby sat down on the grass and closed his eyes, letting the sun's rays warm him.

"Hi."

He opened his eyes and blinked up. Lucky.

"Mr. Niezgocki told me about Thelma. That's great."

"Yeah, and you should have seen her eat the cricket."

"I'm glad, Bobby. I know you were worried about her."

"I feel different today," he said.

"Yeah? Good different or weird different?"

"I don't know. Good different, I guess. It's hard to explain."

"Does that mean you're coming to the Halloween dance?"

"I'll consider it," he said.

They walked across the field. He looked over at the far edge of the rec field, thousands of brilliant leaves fluttering against the blue sky. That morning on TV Roland Prescott had said that the fall foliage was at its peak in terms of colors.

A football bounced on the ground and rolled up to his feet. Bobby picked it up. When he raised his head he saw a bunch of kids coming toward him: Chick Hall, Scott Shanahan, a big kid named Gary Levinson, and several others.

"We need one more to make five on a side," Gary said. "Ballenger, you wanna play?"

"No way!" Chick yelled. "If he plays, I'm

"Go ahead, it's a free country," Gary told him. "We can play four on four."

Chick swore loudly.

"Look, Chick, the bell rings in, like, ten minutes," Gary told him. "You in or out? C'mon, let's get this game rolling."

"Oh, what the . . ." Chick threw up his hands and stomped over next to Scott Shanahan.

"How 'bout it, Ballenger," Gary said. "You playing or not?"

Bobby looked at the football. He felt its solid weight. Its blunt ends. The raised seams under his fingertips.

"Okay," he said, tossing the ball to Gary.

"Okay," Gary said. "We'll take Ballenger, you take Rothrock. One quarterback sneak per series. Four plays, no first downs. You gotta score. We'll kick."

Bobby lined up on the right side of the field. Chick caught the kickoff and ran it back to about the middle of the field. On the first play, Scott tried a short pass but Gary cut in front of the receiver and came up with the ball.

"Interception!"

"Okay, let's stick 'em," Gary said in the huddle. He had a crew cut and long ropy muscles in his arms. "Vinny, take five steps and buttonhook. Justin, do a down-and-out, eight steps, and cut toward the sidelines."

He looked at Bobby.

"I'll do five steps and a quick slant in," Bobby told him. "Give me a pump-fake then look for me long."

"All right, go long and try to get open," Gary said.

"I'll be open," Bobby said. "Just make sure you throw it far enough."

"If you're open, I'll get you the ball," Gary said. "On sixteen."

Bobby lined up as the wide receiver on the right side. Chick lined up in front of him.

"Don't even think about it," Chick said softly.

"Six! Sixty-two!" Gary yelled. "Forty-seven! Sixteen!"

Bobby broke from the line of scrimmage, Chick running right with him. He was a good athlete, fast and agile. *It's not about being fast,* the coach had said last year. *It's about being quick and making the right choice.*

At five steps, Bobby looked right and let his head move right an instant before he cut in toward the middle of the field. The head fake seemed to surprise Chick and throw him off balance for a second. Bobby stopped and whirled around, motioning for the ball. Chick committed himself and lurched forward just as Bobby turned and broke, running full tilt toward the end zone while Chick tried to recover. Bobby ran as fast as he could, figuring Chick for maybe a step and a half behind him, closing fast. He looked back over his left shoulder and saw the ball racing after him in a beautiful arc, tightly spiraling, a friendly UFO humming against the blue sky.

Chick made one last attempt to close the gap, but the ball soared beyond him. Bobby reached out without breaking stride and gathered it in. Touchdown! On the sidelines Lucky had both hands raised.

"Yes!" Gary shouted. "Yes, yes, yes, yes! Put that one on the highlights!"

"Not bad," Bobby told him, high-fiving him. "Not bad at all."

*

After school Dad took him to Exotic Pets. They had several new tarantulas, including a female baboon spider.

"That's one impressive spider," the man said to Dad.

"Yes," Dad said uncertainly. "He seems to have a lot of character. Nice hair, too."

"It's a female," the man said. "Full-grown, she'll be the size of a dinner plate, with her legs spread out."

"No kidding," Dad said.

The baboon spider cost sixty dollars.

"Well?" Dad asked Bobby when the man walked away. "We've still got the money from Mr. Hall. She sure looks healthy—she's even bigger than Monk."

"There will never be another Monk," Bobby said.

"Don't think of it as replacing Monk. Think of

169

it as something different. Something new. What do you think?"

Bobby straightened up and looked at him.

"Dad, I think I want to play football."

"Football?" His father looked at him. "Well, great. You love football."

"No, I mean tackle," Bobby said. "They're going to start a new league for kids twelve through fifteen.

"So what's the problem?"

"It's Mom," Bobby said. "You know she's against tackle football. Says it's too violent, too many injuries. But, I mean, we'll be wearing full equipment, pads, everything. Plus, they have rules so the biggest kids can't carry the ball. It's, like, totally safe."

"I don't have a problem with it, as long as it's well supervised," Dad said. "Why don't you bring it up tonight at supper?"

Sixteen

October 31

Today I read about a kind of parasitic wasp that preys on spiders. It's worse than a horror movie. The wasp flies down and scares the spider so badly it just freezes. Then the wasp lays its eggs on the back of the spider's body. Pretty soon the wasp eggs hatch and tiny larvae start digging down into the spider's body. All this happens while the spider is still alive, trying to go about its business spinning webs and catching bugs, poor thing. The wasp larvae slowly eat the inside organs of the spider until finally the spider is dead. By this time the baby wasps are big enough to leave the spider's empty body and fly away.

Reading this reminded me of how much I hated Chick after he killed Monk. I'd never hated any-

171

body before, and I could feel that hate eating at me like those wasp larvae, from the inside out.

But after Thelma molted, something happened inside me. I don't really understand it, but all of a sudden I didn't hate Chick anymore. We'll never be friends, but I don't hate him, and I guess I'm glad about that. Hating someone all the time takes too much work.

I had another meeting with Miss Davenport yesterday. Said she just wanted to see how I was doing. Miss Davenport said that in a way I owe Chick Hall something because if it wasn't for him I might have stayed in my shell for months, maybe all year. She says Chick made me stand up for who I am.

Maybe. But I don't think I'll send Chick Hall a thank you letter.

I called Mike on Oct. 28 at 4 P.M. Naperville time, just like I promised. It was weird talking to him. On the phone we both were quiet a lot, like we didn't know what to say. I told him all about Thelma molting. Then he told me about a birthday party where some kid's father bought eighteen cases of pop. It sounded funny hearing Mike say pop. Here in New Paltz the kids all say soda.

172

I told Mike all about Monk. He was such a great spider. In sports they're forever talking about how this pitcher or that quarterback has "a lot of heart." Well, Monk had a lot of heart, too.

One day right after I got Monk I almost lost him. I brought him down to the garage thinking I'd let him get some exercise. Big mistake! Monk bolted, took off on me. He just flew across the cement floor. It was like watching a video stuck on fast forward. Monk sped over to the wall and disappeared behind some boxes. The whole time I was cursing myself something fierce. I figured I'd never see him again.

But about five minutes later I found him in back of a box pigging out on a big grasshopper he'd caught himself! I couldn't believe it. It's one thing to eat crickets somebody puts into your cage but Monk went out on his own and hunted down his own food. Wild food. I let Monk spend a few minutes sucking the juice from the grasshopper before I got him back into his cage.

That's how I'll always remember Monk. A true hunter. An Earth Tiger.

I still miss him. I miss that unusual color his hair had when the sun shone on him. I miss the way he looked, all poised and crouched first thing

173

in the morning. He always looked so alert, so ready to take on anything and anyone he would meet.

Thelma's doing great.

After I talked to Mike he mailed me a rubber tarantula that's amazingly realistic, right down to the hairs on the legs. Never seen anything like it.

MOM IS GOING TO LET ME PLAY TACKLE FOOTBALL!!!! First practice in two days—I can't wait!

Last night I went to The Seventh Grade Halloween Dance. Big surprise: I actually had a good time. At first I mostly hung around with Butch at the refreshment table, eating M&Ms and watching kids on the dance floor.

Lots of kids wore Halloween costumes. Lucky says that the great thing about a costume party is that you can be whoever you want. Or you can just be yourself. I decided I'd just be myself.

Miss Terbaldi and Mr. Niezgocki were both there as chaperones. She came dressed as some kind of gypsy; Mr. N came as an alien robot complete with antennaes and flashing lights. One time we saw them dancing together, and it was the strangest dance I'd ever seen.

"They're doing the Monkey," Lucky yelled over the music. We both rolled our eyes at exactly the same moment and started laughing, and then Lucky pulled me out on the dance floor. I was laughing too hard to resist.

But as soon as we got onto the dance floor the fast music turned slow and me and Lucky were slow dancing. It felt funny, like the first time I went rollerskating or skiing. I didn't have any idea what to do, so I just tried to rock back and forth like the other kids and hoped I didn't look too stupid.

Then the DJ put on a fast song and everybody started fast dancing, popping around like grease on a hot griddle. Boy can Lucky dance! I didn't have a clue about what I was doing out there on the dance floor. But so what? I had a blast jumping around to the music along with everybody else.

Seventeen

At 10:30 Saturday morning Butch and Lucky joined Bobby in his bedroom and started hauling out all the boxes he had never gotten around to unpacking. Next they started in on the furniture.

"You won't recognize this place when we're done with it," Lucky said.

"I want to bring Thelma downstairs," Bobby said, pointing to the terrarium. "Butch, can you take the other end?"

"Uh, well . . ." Butch took a step back. "I don't think I should."

"Why not?" Bobby asked.

"Well, see, I had a hernia operation in fourth grade," Butch said. "I'm not supposed to lift anything heavy."

"It's not heavy," Lucky said.

"I can't take any chances," Butch said.

"Oh, brother," Bobby said, bending down again. "Lucky, can you grab the other end?"

During the next hour they carried out furniture, laid down newspapers, and put masking tape along the windows. Finally they were ready to start painting. Butch and Bobby painted the ceiling; Lucky worked on the closet with the built-in shelves.

"What about the walls?" Lucky said. "You pick a color yet?"

"I want them blue, dark blue, but Dad's against it. He wants me to use this extra paint he still has from painting the den. Celery green. The idea of waking up every morning to that . . ."

Bobby mimed putting his finger in his throat and gagging.

"What are you going to do with these shelves?" Lucky asked.

"I got it all planned," Bobby said. "Trilobites on the top shelf, arrowheads on the second one, crystals on the third, snakeskins on the fourth."

"You'll still have four more," Lucky said, pointing. "Down here you could make, like, a gallery for your most terrifying spider photos. That would give Butch nightmares for the rest of his life."

"Very funny," Butch said.

"Well, we wouldn't want to traumatize you or anything." Lucky winked at Bobby.

"I don't know what you're talking about," Butch said.

"Then how come you wouldn't help move the terrarium?"

"Told you. I had a hernia in fourth grade," Butch insisted. "I'm not allowed to lift anything heavy. Doctor's orders."

"Doctor's orders!" Bobby laughed.

"I saw the look on your face," Lucky told Butch. "Like—no way you were going within ten feet of the terrarium!"

"You guys got me dead wrong," Butch said, dipping his brush into the paint. "I love my eight-legged buddies. I am a friend to all spiders."

"Yeah, right," Bobby said. "Ever see an *Arachnophobia*?"

"Saw it twice," Butch retorted. "Liked it even better the second time."

"You lie like a rug," Lucky told him.

Suddenly Bobby started to smile, one of those grins that come from the inside and push out. With an effort he made his expression normal again.

"Hey, you guys hungry?" Bobby asked.

"I am," Lucky said. "Got any munchies?"

"Sure," Bobby said. "How 'bout a sandwich? We've got lunch meat. Ham. Turkey, I think."

"Turkey with a little mayo," Butch said. "See if you got any chips."

"Ham," Lucky said. "Wheat bread. No mustard, no mayo."

He skipped downstairs. Mom and Breezy were

178

drinking coffee in the kitchen. Bobby took out six slices of bread.

"How's it coming up there?" Mom asked.

"Great," he said. "You're really going to be surprised."

"Not too surprised, I hope."

He went into the den and opened the closet door. Inside a small box, he found the rubber tarantula Mike had sent him. It was big, hairy, and even more realistic than Bobby remembered. A heart-stopper all the way. He brought it back into the kitchen. While Mom and Breezy watched, he put two slices of turkey on top of one piece of white bread. He put the other piece of bread on top, and the rubber spider on top of the bread.

"Oh, God," Mom said. "You're not going to do that, are you?"

"What do you expect?" Breezy asked cheerfully. "He's a pre-adolescent boy."

"Very funny," he said.

"I'm serious," Breezy replied. "This is considered normal behavior for a boy your age."

"Butch says he's got no fear of spiders," Bobby said. "Well, I want to prove it, one way or another, so I'm conducting a little experiment. Don't get freaked out if you hear a scream."

"This is reminding me," Breezy said, "of another stunt you pulled."

Bobby grinned as he wrapped each sandwich

in a napkin. He wrote an H on his sandwich and on Lucky's. On Butch's sandwich he wrote a T.

"Is that a T for turkey?" Mom asked. "Or tarantula?"

"Take your pick," Bobby said. He loaded the sandwiches, three glasses of milk, a bowl of chips, and a dozen cookies onto a large tray.

"You're absolutely terrible," Mom said.

"I know," he replied.

"Listen, don't stay up there too long," Mom said. "Those paint fumes can do a number on you. Open the windows."

"Okay, okay." He lifted the tray and started up the stairs.

"Are you going out later on?" Mom called.

"Nope, I'll be home," he said, carefully balancing the tray so he didn't spill anything. *Home*. The word echoed in the staircase, and in a space inside him. For the first time in a long time it sounded like the right word.